Disney

PETER PAN & WENDY

DISNEY
PETER PAN & WENDY

THE

JUNIOR NOVELIZATION

Adapted by ELIZABETH RUDNICK

DISNEP PRESS

LOS ANGELES • NEW YORK

Copyright © 2023 Disney Enterprises, Inc.

All rights reserved. Published by Disney Press, an imprint of Buena Vista
Books, Inc. No part of this book may be reproduced or transmitted
in any form or by any means, electronic or mechanical, including
photocopying, recording, or by any information storage and retrieval
system, without written permission from the publisher.
For information address Disney Press, 1200 Grand Central Avenue,
Glendale, California 91201.

Printed in the United States of America
First Paperback Edition, January 2023
1 3 5 7 9 10 8 6 4 2
FAC-025438-22322

Library of Congress Control Number: 2022939142
ISBN 978-1-368-08045-3

Visit disneybooks.com

SUSTAINABLE
FORESTRY
INITIATIVE
Certified Chain of Custody
Promoting Sustainable Forestry
www.sfiprogram.org
SFI-01054
The SFI label applies to the text stock

CHAPTER ONE

On a quiet street in London, a sea of umbrellas made its way down the cobblestoned streets as men and women returned home under a rapidly darkening sky. Thunder pealed and the rain grew steadier. The occasional carriage moved by, the clip-clop of the horse's hooves echoing off the stone houses and sending splashes of water up onto the sidewalk. One by one, people moved off the sidewalk, ducking into the modest but well-cared-for homes, whose warm light glowed welcomingly.

In one such home, the Darling house, the thunder could not be heard over the epic battle currently playing out.

Brandishing wooden swords, John and Michael Darling raced down the main hallway of their home. The family dog, a big Saint Bernard named Nana, nipped at their heels. She tried, though often failed, to keep the boys under control. It was how she had earned her name: the nana of the group. But sometimes she couldn't help joining in. Back and forth their swords flew, narrowly missing any items that happened to be in arm's reach.

Portraits of their family through the years rattled and shook on the walls. Outside, a bolt of lightning illuminated the sky, followed by a clap of thunder, giving the fight a more ominous feel. The rain pounded on the roof. But despite the noise, or perhaps spurred on by it, their fight continued.

"Your time is running out, Peter Pan!" John shouted, waving his wooden sword in the air. At ten years old, John considered himself the far superior swordsman. Tipping his head, but not enough to dislodge his father's top hat, which he had "borrowed" for the game, John took several quick steps forward.

His younger brother, Michael, jumped back, clutching his well-worn stuffed bear in his hands as he tried to evade his brother's swinging sword.

The game was one they had played many times before. But it never ceased to amuse them. Peter Pan was the star of one of their favorite bedtime stories, and they loved pretending to be the boy who never grew up. Well, Michael enjoyed playing Peter. John preferred to be the villainous Captain Hook.

"Watch out for the crocodile!" John shouted, caught up in the game.

Nana let out a warning bark, as if noticing a real live crocodile herself. But Michael shook his head. "Peter isn't afraid of crocodiles," he said, more than happy to correct his older brother. "*You* are!"

Both boys roared, and they continued their fight, moving

through the hallway of their cozy townhome. The rain got louder as they chased each other up the spiral staircase. But it wasn't loud enough to drown out the huff of their older sister, Wendy, as she stormed out of her parents' bedroom. She was clutching a suitcase in one hand. Her cheeks were red, and her light brown hair was disheveled.

"I heard you the first time!" she said as she stomped up the stairs, right in front of her brothers. "I'll be ready."

Not looking at John or Michael, she made her way up the stairs and then through the open door of the nursery. The lofty attic space was the room for all three children. Toys were scattered across the floor, and three beds were spaced apart—two against one wall, a third on the opposite. Across from the door, taking up most of the far wall, was a large window, complete with a cozy window seat.

After throwing her suitcase on the window seat, Wendy began to toss clothes inside. Behind her, she heard her brothers enter the room, and the sound of their clashing swords caused her frown to deepen. Could she not have a moment's peace, to sulk as she deserved?

She sighed. She knew her face and mood matched the gloomy, rainy weather outside. She couldn't believe that this was her last night in the nursery. She had tried so hard to convince her mother and father that she didn't need to go to boarding school, but they insisted. It was the "right" thing to do for her future.

But how could it be right if it felt so terribly wrong? She didn't want to leave her home. She paused, clutching a stuffed animal to her chest. She wasn't ready to give up her childhood and all the fun that went with it—like, she thought as she heard John and Michael battling behind her, playing pretend.

She smiled. Sure, she had to move out the next day. But that didn't mean she couldn't enjoy one last fight with her brothers. Whirling around, she gave John and Michael a wicked grin.

"You haven't forgotten about *me*, have you?" she asked.

She grabbed a sword of her own and leapt into the fray. The boys' faces lit up as their sister joined in the fun. But then, just as quickly, they became serious again. The fight would go on—even better than before.

Not wasting a moment, Wendy nodded at her youngest brother. "Give me that treasure!" she shouted. She grabbed a pair of pearl earrings he clutched in his hands. "Now . . . leave Hook to me!"

She turned to John and crouched, ready to pounce. "Make way, Captain Hook, lest I run you through."

She and John began to duel. Lost in the action, Wendy forgot about why she was sad. True, they had played this game too many times to count, and she might have grown a bit too old for it. But still she never tired of it.

As she swung her sword harder and harder at her little brother, John's expression changed from delighted to wary.

Suddenly, she lunged, hitting his knuckles—hard—with her sword.

"Ow!" John said.

"What's that?" Wendy said, still caught up in the game. "Are you giving up?"

"No, you're just—"

Before John could finish, Wendy brought her sword down on his, knocking it out of his hand. It flew across the room and into a mirror hanging on the wall. There was a loud crack as the sword crashed into the mirror, shattering it.

The children's eyes widened, and their swords dropped. Nana whimpered softly.

Wendy lowered her sword and gulped. "Oops."

The door to the nursery swung open. Mr. Darling strode into the room. He was fixing his bow tie, with his fingers moving in well-practiced motion. "All right, children, time for—"

He saw all three of his children staring, guiltily, at the wall behind him. Turning, he spotted the broken mirror. He sighed.

"Not again!" he said. "Who is responsible for this?"

The children looked at the floor, their lips sealed. They had been through this before. It was as much a part of the game as the battle itself. Pirates never told on other pirates. Unfortunately, while they didn't say anything, John's quick glance at Wendy was all Mr. Darling needed.

Mr. Darling approached his eldest. "Wendy."

Wendy's head snapped up, and she looked at her brothers. "Tattletale!"

"I didn't say anything!" countered John.

"*You* two started it!" she said. Looking back at her father, she added, "It was *their* game. It's *their* fault and—"

"Enough!" Mr. Darling snapped, stopping Wendy instantly. He held out his hand. "Swords. Now."

Reluctantly, Wendy and Michael turned over their wooden weapons. Mr. Darling raised an eyebrow.

"Hat," he added. John slowly reached up, removed his father's hat from his head, and handed it over. Mr. Darling wasn't done yet, though. He knew that this game also involved a certain item of his. "Watch."

John pulled the watch out of his pocket, his lips trembling. "But it helps me sleep," he said, no longer sounding like a mean pirate captain but instead very much like a ten-year-old boy.

"It helps you—" Mr. Darling stopped when he saw his son's face. "Oh, very well. Just be *very careful* with it. A man's timepiece is of the utmost importance. Just like his house . . ." He walked to the broken mirror and picked up the sword that lay under it. He sighed again. "Although I'm afraid ours will be nothing but ruins by the time the three of you are grown."

Nana thumped her tail on the hardwood floor as she looked back and forth between the children and Mr. Darling.

"Come along, Nana," Mr. Darling said.

"Oh, but can't she just stay for—" Wendy started.

Mr. Darling cut her off. "No, she cannot. Honestly, Wendy, is this really how you want to spend your last night at home?"

Wendy frowned at the reminder of her situation. "We were just having a bit of fun!"

"Exactly!" Mr. Darling said. "You are too old for this to be the type of fun you're having."

Without another word, he took Nana by the collar and led her out the door. They disappeared down the stairs, leaving the children alone.

There was an awkward silence as the three stood in their room, unsure what to do or say.

"Why did you do that?" John finally asked.

Wendy shrugged. "You're a pirate, aren't you? Every man for himself."

She wasn't entirely sure why she had done any of it: joining in the fight, talking back to her father, telling on her brothers. She was just tired of it all and furious that the next day, a new life was being forced on her. She clenched her fists tightly and felt a small prick. Opening one of her hands, she saw that she was still holding the earrings she had taken as "treasure."

Walking to the broken mirror on her side of the nursery— separated from the boys' half by a curtain—she held the earrings up to her ears. She tilted her head just a bit so that her face was split in two by the crack. Briefly, she felt like she was looking at two Wendys—the one who wanted to stay in the nursery forever and the other, smaller Wendy who was curious what adventures the grown-up world held.

"They suit you, Wendy."

Mrs. Darling's voice startled Wendy. She whipped around, dropping her hands from her ears.

"You should take them with you," Mrs. Darling went on, entering the nursery. She was dressed for an evening out and, as always, looked the picture of refined elegance. Wendy didn't know how her mother did it, but there was never a hair out of place or a wrinkle to mar the fabric of her dress.

"I'd rather not," Wendy snapped, flouncing away from the mirror and dropping onto her bed.

Mrs. Darling gently parted the curtains that divided the room and then sat down on the bed beside Wendy.

"You really must set a better example for your brothers, though," she said. "They look up to you so much."

"That's what they have *you* for," Wendy said, pouting.

Mrs. Darling smiled and brushed a strand of hair off her daughter's face. "They need *me* to be their mother, and your father to be their father. But they need *you* to be their big sister. They will follow your lead—so you must be a good leader."

"How am I supposed to do that from boarding school?" Wendy said.

"By going with your head held high, to begin with," Mrs.

Darling answered. "This is just what we do. If a young lady is lucky enough, at a certain age, she goes off to school, to get ready for the life ahead of her."

Wendy shook her head. "What if I don't want that life?"

"It's what *I* did when I was your age."

"What if I don't want your life?" Wendy snapped. How could her mother understand? Did she even remember how it felt to be Wendy's age? To always be told what to do and how to do it?

Mrs. Darling's eyes shimmered with emotion, but her voice remained even as she spoke. "What is it that you are afraid of?"

At the question, Wendy's anger faded and was replaced with sadness. "I want things to stay the way they are."

"The way they are?" Mrs. Darling repeated. She pointed to the end of the bed, where Wendy's feet hung over. "You scarcely fit in your bed!"

Wendy pulled her feet up, not willing to admit that this was true.

"You're growing up," said Mrs. Darling.

"Perhaps I don't want to grow up," said Wendy.

Mrs. Darling nodded. She knew no one liked the idea of change. "You can't stop time, Wendy," she said. "It'll march on whether you like it or not. Just think of all the things you would miss out on if you didn't see where it took you!" She paused, hoping to see some sort of acceptance in Wendy's eyes. But the girl's expression remained hard, and she turned on her side. "And

9

imagine what the world would miss out on if *you* weren't there to do them."

Wendy didn't speak. Gently, Mrs. Darling pulled up the blanket and smoothed it over her daughter's trembling shoulders, then ran her fingers through her daughter's hair. As all three children lay down in their beds, Mrs. Darling sang them a gentle lullaby, the same one she sang every night. Soon Wendy and her brothers were fast asleep.

Leaning over, Mrs. Darling kissed Wendy atop her head. Then she tiptoed toward the door, pulling the curtains that separated Wendy's bed from the boys' shut behind her.

"Good night, children," she said to their sleeping forms before leaving the room and closing the nursery door behind her.

CHAPTER TWO

The nursery grew quiet, save for the occasional rustle of sheets when the children turned in their sleep. The house seemed to sense its inhabitants' resting, and the creaking of floorboards hushed as the foundation, too, settled in for the night.

Suddenly, a gentle but unmistakable sound of bells, just outside the rain-streaked window, broke the silence. If any of the children had been awake and looked outside, they would have been surprised to see a small light that brightened as it pushed the window open and flew into the nursery.

The light, however, was truly a rather small fairy: Tinker Bell.

Only a few inches high, the petite creature flitted around the room, with her large brown eyes scanning the space. Golden flecks of dust shimmered on her dark curls, and on her back, a pair of translucent wings flapped so quickly they were barely visible. Moving across the room, she looked down on John and then Michael. She frowned. They were not what she was looking for. Turning, she spotted some curtains pulled across the far end of

the room. Curious, she flew over and waved her hands. Gold dust flew from her fingers, and the curtains magically pulled aside, revealing Wendy Darling.

Tinker Bell's eyes lit up. *This* was who she had been looking for! Moving closer, she blew a kiss in Wendy's direction. Another gust of shimmery dust appeared. As the pixie dust landed on Wendy's skin, it made her sparkle ever so slightly, and for a moment, she and Tinker Bell both lit up the room. Then Wendy smiled in her sleep. Tinker Bell nodded. The pixie dust was doing its job, lulling Wendy deeper into happy dreams.

Then, as Tinker Bell watched, Wendy began to float.

This was precisely what Tinker Bell had been hoping would happen. The happy dreams and the pixie dust combined were working their magic. She clasped her hands together, eager to enact the rest of her plan. . . .

"Gotcha!"

A hand snatched Tinker Bell from the air.

Wendy's eyes flew open. She looked up. And then she looked down. Seeing that she was not on her bed, she let out a shout and flung her arms into the air. All happy thoughts gone, she crashed onto the ground with a thud.

"What . . . what was happening?" she asked, utterly confused. "Was I dreaming?"

John had grabbed the new arrival, and Michael had woken up, too.

"You were *flying*!" said the younger boy.

"How?" Wendy asked.

"A little bug did it," Michael answered as though that made perfect sense and was something that happened every day. He pointed to his older brother, who sat with his back to the window and his hands cupped around Tinker Bell.

"I'm not sure it's a bug . . ." he said. Inside his cupped palms, he felt whatever it was flittering against his fingers. It reminded him of catching a firefly on a warm summer night and keeping it for a moment before setting it free. The flickering was gentle, like a tickle. He parted his fingers just enough so that Michael and Wendy could take a peek.

Tinker Bell stared at them, her face red with anger. Wendy jumped back, unsure what to do. None of this made sense.

"It's a . . ." Wendy struggled to find the words. "A . . ."

Before she could finish, a shiny blade emerged from the darkness behind John and landed on the boy's shoulder. John froze. This blade was cold steel—nothing like the wooden swords he and his siblings played with.

"*She* is a fairy," a voice said, "and you'll do well to unhand her."

John did not hesitate. He opened his hands, and the fairy, as the voice had called her, flew to her freedom. As she hovered in the air, a noise that sounded like a million windchimes ringing all at once filled the room. Tinker Bell shook her head and waved

her finger at them. Her meaning was clear: *Never call me a bug again!*

Meanwhile, the figure holding the sword emerged from the shadows into the dim light of the room. It was a boy around Wendy's age. His brown skin was covered by clothes the colors of the forest, and underneath the feathered cap on his head, a mischievous spark glinted in his eyes.

The children couldn't believe what they were seeing. But there was no doubt in their minds . . .

"Are you . . ." John started.

"Peter Pan?" Michael finished.

The boy cocked his head. "Were you expecting someone else?"

Wendy, finally finding her voice, stepped in front of her younger brothers. "We weren't expecting anyone at all," she said firmly. "How are you real? Aren't you just a bedtime story?"

Peter shrugged. "Why can't I be both? I like hearing stories about myself. And your mother is very good at telling them."

Wendy's eyes narrowed. Peter had answered one of her questions, but she had more. Namely . . . "What are you doing here?"

Peter looked around the room. Then he lowered his voice. "Two things," he said. "One: we have to get you of here. And two . . ." His voice trailed off as across the room, Tinker Bell chimed from atop a chest of drawers. She gestured to the chest

and made a few more chimes. Then, as they all watched, the drawers shook violently.

"My shadow!" Peter finished his thought.

"Your shadow?" John repeated.

Peter nodded. "I knew I left it here."

The Darling children exchanged looks. He had been there before? When? How?

Unaware that the children were silently questioning everything, Peter went on. "It's always trying to get away, and I've only got the one. . . ."

He ran to the dresser and pulled open the bottom drawer. As he did so, the slightly ajar middle drawer slammed shut. Peter grabbed for it and pulled it open only to have the top drawer open and hit him right on the head.

"*Ow!*" Peter cried, rubbing his forehead.

Just then, a shadow—Peter's shadow!—rose on the wall behind him. It was the oddest shadow any of the children had ever seen. It did not go where Peter went. It didn't lengthen or shorten based on the slant of the light. It acted with a mind of its own. In fact, as they looked on, it appeared to crouch down and slink along the wall, as if it might sneak away.

Spotting the mischievous shadow, Tinker Bell chimed frantically.

Alerted by Tinker Bell's chimes, Peter turned in her direction. Then he cried out. "There you are!"

Peter leapt into the air behind it, chasing it across the room and straight into Wendy's closet. He landed with a loud crash.

As Peter struggled back to his feet, the shadow continued trying to escape. It leapt out of the closet, past Wendy, and then shrunk to the size of a doll and zipped right into a large dollhouse that was set up in the corner of the room. Following fast on its shadowy heels, Tinker Bell flew through one of the tiny windows. A yellow glow lit up the dollhouse as the fairy chased the shadow from one floor to the next.

Wendy watched, her eyes wide and her mind racing. She tried to make sense of everything she was seeing, but it was near impossible. And now her own brother was getting involved. Michael and Peter lifted the dollhouse up and over, shaking it.

"Get out of there, shadow!" Michael yelled.

The shadow leapt free and continued its frantic race across the room. It sped over the ceiling and then, before any of them could stop it, slipped out the nursery door and into the stairwell. Wendy's hand went to her mouth. If the shadow were to get out of the house, there was no telling if they would ever be able to catch it. Pushing her brothers in front of her, Wendy followed the shadow into the hall. Scanning the dark space, they spotted the shadow making its way down the stairs.

But before it could get to the bottom landing, Nana pounced out of the dark and landed right on the shadow's toes. The

shadow, never having encountered a dog before, became instantly still, then began to tremble in terror.

"Good job, Nana!" Wendy said.

Nana's tail wagged, and the shadow wriggled and squirmed.

Peter ran down the steps and grabbed a hold of his shadow, yanking it away from Nana. "When are you going to learn you can't get anywhere without me?" Peter asked.

The shadow gestured to the stairwell and shrugged as if to say, *I've gotten pretty far, actually.*

But Peter shook his head. "That time doesn't count," he said, sounding a little like a pouty boy rather than the daring adventurer he was in the bedtime stories the Darlings loved so much.

With a huff, Peter sat down on the stairs and tried to tie the shadow to his foot. But the shadow was as slippery as an eel, and Peter could not get a firm hold. His eyebrows knitted together and his mouth turned down as he struggled.

"Come on, hold still . . ." he said.

Wendy felt a rush of sympathy. He was trying so hard, and clearly it was upsetting. She rushed back into the nursery and grabbed a small bag from the bureau before going to sit beside Peter on the top step.

"Maybe I can help you with that?" she asked, reaching into the bag and lifting out a small sewing needle and a spool of thread. Seeing the sharp needle, Tinker Bell flew to the rescue, pushing Wendy's hands to try to move them farther from Peter.

Peter stopped her. "It's okay, Tink," he said. "Wendy won't hurt me."

"Can't she speak?" Wendy asked as she watched the fairy weigh Peter's words and then back away.

"Of course she can," Peter said. "You just haven't learned to hear her right."

Tinker Bell chimed her agreement.

Wendy looked at the little creature: Tinker Bell's expression spoke volumes. Though Wendy couldn't understand the fairy language, she liked the sound of it just the same. "You're very small, Tinker Bell," she said kindly.

Tinker Bell instantly began to chime and jingle. It went on for quite a while. Even though she couldn't speak fairy, Wendy could tell she had offended Tinker Bell in some way. "What's she saying?" she asked.

Peter shrugged. "She says: All fairies are small. That's what makes them fairies."

Wendy looked back and forth between Peter and Tink. It was clear that was not at all what the fairy had said, and Peter either had made it up or was nervous to tell Wendy the truth. Wendy suspected the latter when Tinker Bell knocked over a toy soldier.

There was nothing Wendy could do about the misunderstanding quite yet, so she got to work. She threaded the needle and began to sew the shadow to Peter's foot. The needle moved smoothly in and out of the shadow, as if it were a piece of black

velvet. Wendy's fingers hesitated. She was both fascinated and a little disturbed by what she was doing. She had never sewn a shadow before, and while it made no sense, it seemed to work.

As she continued with her task, Wendy asked a question that had been tickling the back of her brain. "How did you know my name, Peter Pan?"

Peter's eyes stayed glued to the needle. "I heard your mother call you," he said. "'Wendy, time to wake up! Wendy, time for school!' But you never want to go."

Wendy's hand stilled. While it perhaps should have bothered her that this boy knew so much, it didn't. In fact, she found herself moved in a strange way. Peter Pan seemed to understand exactly what she had been feeling in her heart.

"You've been watching me?" Wendy said.

Peter nodded. "Sometimes."

"Why?"

"Because," Peter answered, "I've been waiting for you to say it."

Wendy cocked her head. "Say what?"

Peter finally lifted his eyes from where the shadow was being attached. There was a mischievous glint to his eyes, but his voice was serious as he said, "The same thing I said once upon a time: *I don't want to grow—*"

As Wendy got caught up in what Peter was saying, her finger

slipped and the needle pricked Peter's foot. It wasn't hard or deep. Yet he shouted as though Wendy had fatally wounded him.

Flitting forward, Tinker Bell knocked the needle from Wendy's hand. She chimed angrily as she turned toward Peter. The boy held his foot in his hand, his face pained.

Wendy gulped. Had she really hurt him?

CHAPTER THREE

"**Y**ou stabbed me!" Peter Pan shouted. "You stabbed me in the heart!"

His shadow, hopping all around, didn't help the situation.

John and Michael, who had been watching the whole thing with a great deal of curiosity, looked down at Peter's foot.

"Your heart's in your foot?" John asked, a bit confused.

Peter nodded. "Isn't yours?"

"I'm sorry!" said Wendy. "What can I do?"

Moaning, Peter massaged his foot and made sad faces. He stood up and made a big show of how painful it was. Wendy began to wonder if she really had hurt him, though she really didn't see how. . . .

Trying to be helpful, Michael followed Peter as he hopped back into the nursery. "When Mr. Bear gets hurt, Mama gives him a kiss to make it better."

Peter looked down at the little boy. "What's a . . . kiss?"

"**You don't know what a kiss is?**" Wendy asked, surprised.

Her mother and father had been giving her kisses ever since she could remember. It was one way she knew they loved her—even if sometimes she got mad at them.

Peter shook his head.

Wendy hesitated. *She* knew what a kiss was, true, but she wasn't sure she was ready to show Peter a real one. She grabbed a thimble from her sewing kit and handed it to him.

"Here," she said. "*This* is a kiss."

The boy looked down at the thimble in his hand. He turned it over and around as though it were a strange and unknown artifact. Finally he looked up and smiled. "I like it very much," he said.

Wendy nodded. "And now do you feel better?"

"Yes. Good as new," Peter answered.

Tinker Bell flew to Peter and began to chime impatiently in his ear. Peter listened, or seemed to listen, and then nodded in apparent agreement. He stood up and stretched, making sure his shadow stayed with him.

"What's she saying?" Wendy asked, looking closely at Tinker Bell. The little fairy's eyebrows were furrowed, and she did not seem at all pleased.

"That it's high time we go," Peter answered.

"Go where?" said John.

Peter smiled like a little boy with a surprise. "To the one place in the entire universe where you can really be yourself," he said

with glee in his voice. "Where the greatest adventures are right around every corner. Where there are no rules, no schools, no bedtimes, no mothers and fathers . . . and most of all . . ."

"No growing up," Wendy finished.

"That most of all," said Peter.

She knew exactly what he was talking about. After all, for ages she had grown up hearing stories about the boy and this place. Her face lit with excitement as she clapped her hands. "You're talking about Neverland!"

John's eyes widened behind his glasses. "Surely *we* couldn't go there, though. . . ."

Going to Neverland would be a dream come true, but John liked a good plan—and this all seemed rather unplanned.

"Of course you could!" Peter said.

John gulped.

"But how do you get there?" Michael asked.

A wicked grin spread across Peter's face. "*That's* the fun part."

Moments later, the Darling children had moved to stand on the ledge outside their nursery. Above them, the sky had cleared and stars sparkled. In the small yard below, Nana, who had raced down the stairs when the children had begun packing, looked up at them and barked nervously.

It had taken them no time to gather what they needed

for Neverland—shoes for Wendy, Mr. Bear for Michael, and their father's top hat and an umbrella for John. Now they were ready . . . sort of.

Looking at the ground, which seemed awfully far below, John gulped again. "Well, *this* suddenly seems like a terrible idea."

Wendy was not nearly as bothered by the height. "I've always dreamed of flying," she said happily.

Standing next to her, Peter nodded. "It's the easiest thing in the world. All you have to do is fill your head with happy thoughts."

Suspicious, John narrowed his eyes. "That's it?"

Hovering in the air beside Peter, Tinker Bell chimed. "Oh, right," Peter said. "And a little pixie dust."

Tinker Bell flew to Wendy and chimed again. Wendy did her best to understand, but once more, she couldn't figure out what the little fairy was telling her to do. Sighing, Tinker Bell brushed her little hand down over Wendy's eyes.

"You want me to close my eyes?" Wendy asked.

Tink nodded, and Wendy squished her eyes closed. She did her very best to think happy thoughts. But at first, nothing came.

"What are you thinking of?" Peter asked from somewhere close by.

Wendy hesitated. What *was* she thinking about? It was all vague moments. She needed to focus.

"Of when I was little," she finally said, "when I was happy . . . of how things used to be."

And just like that, memories began to take shape behind her closed eyes. She thought about walking through the park with her mother, about Christmas morning, about playing with Nana as a puppy. The happy thoughts continued to flood her mind. Piano lessons with her father, mud fights with her brothers in the backyard, afternoons spent curling up in her mother's arms as the daylight turned golden . . .

As she concentrated, Tinker Bell covered her with pixie dust. It sparkled in the air around her, and for a moment, she appeared golden herself as she slowly lifted off the ledge into the air.

Her eyes still closed, Wendy didn't know what was happening until Peter said, "Now. Open your eyes!"

Wendy did—and gasped. She was floating high in the air, with her house below, as if she had stayed in the same place and the world had slipped down beneath her feet. The buildings, which seemed so tall when she was on the ground, now looked like the toys in her dollhouse, tiny and quaint. A smile on her face, Wendy watched as her brothers followed her into the air, leaving trails of pixie dust in their wake.

"Whoaaaa . . ." Michael said, clutching his bear to his chest. He let out another happy shout and dipped down and then back up. Beside him, John kicked his legs nervously in the air.

"Are you certain it's safe?" he asked.

Peter smiled. "Of course it is! I haven't fallen yet!"

John shot the boy a look. That wasn't the most reassuring of answers.

Laughing good-naturedly at her brother's concern, Wendy continued to explore her new freedom. As she spun herself in the air, joy welled up inside her.

"I can fly!" she shouted.

And as the feeling intensified, she soared upward and then dove down, her stomach flipping and flopping with the sensation. Racing past her brothers, she flew a bit farther into the city, touching down on the roof of a townhouse here, hopping off another townhouse there.

"Come on!" she called out, motioning for her brothers to follow as she leapt from the roof of one building to another, and they moved farther and farther from their own home. Together, they made their way over the city. It seemed almost magical from their vantage point, with the usual drab grays and blacks of the buildings, and the covering of smoke and soot, appearing radiant blue and deep gold. It was as though somehow Tinker Bell's pixie dust had covered not just them but all of London.

Wendy finally came to a stop on the face of Big Ben. The large clock tower was one of the most recognizable landmarks in London. And here she was, just standing on it as though she were on the sidewalk. Then Peter swooped in and landed beside her.

Michael came to a rather bumpy stop on the opposite side of the clockface, smiling widely, while John popped open his umbrella and slowly descended until his feet gently hit the stone surface. When they had all caught their breath, Peter pointed up to two stars twinkling in the sky.

"There it is," he said. "Second star to the right and straight on till morning."

"It looks very far away," Michael said, clutching Mr. Bear to his chest.

John looked down at his watch. He frowned. He was certainly not used to being up this late, let alone up and flying. "We should probably go some other time. . . ."

Wendy shook her head. What was wrong with her brothers? This was their chance to do something amazing—and they were worried about rules. Well, not her.

"I'm ready!" she said, frowning at the boys. "I'm ready to go to Neverland. Let's go right now!"

"But what about Mother and Father?" John asked.

Peter brushed off the boy's worry. "We'll be back before they wake up. Before morning! Time works differently in Neverland." Just then, the minute hand on Big Ben moved backward. "It goes up and down and backwards and forwards. . . ."

Now both hands began moving, in opposite directions. The world around them began to shimmer and then change in front of their very eyes. The night sky seemed to stretch and shift around them, like the fabric of space and time was opening up. It was the most magical thing Wendy had ever seen.

Holding out her arms, she looked at her brothers. "John . . . Michael . . . take my hands."

The boys hesitated and then slowly slipped their hands into hers.

"What do you say?" she asked. "Ready for an adventure?"

John shook his head at the same time Michael nodded.

"Doesn't Mother always say you need to be the responsible one?" John asked, his voice shaking a little.

Wendy grinned and nodded at the clock tower behind them. "Too late!" she said.

She jumped into the night air. And just like that, London vanished beneath their feet.

They were off to Neverland.

CHAPTER FOUR

The air around them seemed to soften as Wendy, John, and Michael followed Peter. The stars pulsed and then turned to colorful streaks. As Wendy watched, the streaks began to twirl, the colors growing more and more vibrant until they vanished and the space around them darkened. There was no up. There was no down. Everything seemed to float in this void between worlds. John's pocket watch drifted out of his vest and he grabbed it back—the hands spinning wildly as though trying to find the time.

In what seemed like only a moment, Wendy found herself in a whole new world. Beneath her, a crystal-clear ocean stretched out, turning pink and gold as the water reflected the rays of the rising sun. Wendy looked up and saw morning light rippling through the sky to where a shadow of land blossomed on the horizon, growing larger as they flew closer.

"Look!" Michael said beside Wendy.

"I see it!" Wendy shouted back.

John, who had pushed his hat down over his eyes to avoid

the whirly, twirly race through the air, finally pushed it up. "Is that..."

"Neverland!" Peter finished with a huge smile on his face as he looked out over his home.

Neverland was like nothing Wendy could have imagined and everything she could have wished. Rocky outcroppings lined the shore, creating hollows where mermaids played and splashed. Beyond the rocks, towering cliffs soared into the air and then gave way to hills the color of emeralds. Swooping down, Wendy found herself over a field of golden grass that rose and fell like waves.

"Come on!" Peter said, flying up beside her. "There's more!"

Taking off, Peter flew up, up, up. Wendy followed as fast as she could, her brothers a bit more slowly. While she was infatuated with this new world, they were still worried. It seemed like it was all just a little too perfect. They had heard the stories of Peter Pan. They knew that wherever he went, there was one person who was sure to follow.

So where, they couldn't help wondering as they raced behind Wendy and Peter, was Captain Hook?

Skylight stood alone in the crow's nest of the *Jolly Roger*. The large pirate ship's sails were tied tight to the mast, ready to be unfurled at a moment's notice. But right then, things were calm. The

wind was still, the sun was shining, and as he used his spyglass to scan the sky, he saw nothing out of the ordinary. Just birds in the trees, mermaids playing in the water, Peter Pan flying through the air . . .

Wait! What?

Skylight readjusted his spyglass and gulped. Sure enough, there was Peter Pan.

"Oh, no," he said. "Oh, no, no no." This wasn't good. This wasn't good at all.

Skylight jumped from the crow's nest and swung out over the deck of the ship. The intimidating pirate ship had seen better days. Its sides were crusted with barnacles, and the wood of its decks was rotten. A large white flag fluttered in the breeze, making the hand-painted skull and crossbones bend eerily and telling all who saw the *Jolly Roger* that they should fear its crew.

Landing, Skylight tried not to step on the piles of sleeping pirates that covered the deck. His crewmates were a grungy bunch. There were Gurley and Old Clemson; the always cranky Mrs. Starkey; and Dirtbag Benny, who had gotten his name because he was quite filthy—even for a pirate. Then there were Scrimshaw Sam and the biggest of them all, Bill Jukes.

Running past them now, Skylight whispered to himself, "He's back, he's back. The boy is back!"

His words, while hushed, managed to rouse the pirates, and they slowly began to stir as Skylight made his way to the captain's

quarters. He stopped in front of the door. It, like the rest of the ship, was sorely in need of repair. It was covered in scratches, and holes had been patched over but remained splintery. Skylight took a deep breath. Then he knocked.

Nobody answered.

Skylight knocked again.

"What is it?"

The voice that came from the other side of the door was deep and raspy. And it didn't sound at all pleased to be interrupted.

Gulping, Skylight looked over his shoulder at the rest of the pirates. They were all watching him with nervous anticipation.

"It's the boy, Cap'n," he said shakily. "It's Peter Pan."

Suddenly, a loud boom echoed through the air, and the door flew off its hinges. It hit Skylight square on the chest and sent him flying backward. He landed on the deck with a thud, knocked unconscious.

As the smoke cleared, a man emerged from the blackness of the quarters like some kind of monster from a child's worst nightmare. His hair was dark like the smoke through which he walked, and a heavy mustache covered his top lip. His eyes were cold and his skin hardened by years under the sun. And where his right hand should have been, there was a big rusty hook.

This was Captain James Hook.

"Never. Say. His name," he snarled.

A cold wind accompanied his icy words, and as it traveled over

the deck, the pirates felt a chill run down their spines. Unaware, or perhaps simply used to the effect he had on his crew, the captain turned toward his quarters and shouted, "Mr. Smee! Make a note. My cabin needs a new door."

A moment later, Mr. Smee emerged from the cabin as well. The older pirate was stooped at the shoulder with age; his hair— what was left of it—was the same gray as his beard. A pair of spectacles sat atop his nose, and an ear horn dangled around his neck, since, after years of standing beside firing cannons, he'd become a tad hard of hearing. Approaching the captain, Mr. Smee nodded. An apron covered his usual striped shirt, and he held a mixing bowl. The captain had interrupted him in the middle of making breakfast.

"A new door!" Mr. Smee said. "Yes. Right. Mightn't I say, Cap'n, that'll be your third this month."

Captain Hook shrugged. All he cared about was that blasted Peter Pan. "And it shan't be my last. Where is my spyglass?"

Mr. Smee, not wearing his ear horn, misheard and handed him a sea bass. The captain quickly threw it to the ground.

"*Spyglass!*" he repeated, louder.

"Ah, spyglass!" Mr. Smee said. "At hand, Cap'n."

He produced the requested item, which was quickly snatched from his grasp.

"Speak not to me of hands," Hook snarled. Then he shook the spyglass open and trained it on the sky. At first he could

see nothing but the irritatingly blue sky and bright sun, which seemed to mock him with its happiness and warmth. But then a streak flew by. Following with his spyglass, Captain Hook spotted Peter. He saw that the boy's little fairy was with him as always, but surprisingly, there seemed to be three new children in tow.

"Aye. There you are," the captain said like a hunter spotting its prey. "Footloose and flying free . . . but not for long."

Lowering the spyglass, the man sighed. His morning was officially ruined. But perhaps there was a way to change that.

Seeing the gleam in his captain's eyes, Mr. Smee spoke up. He never knew what to expect when Peter Pan was involved. "What would you have us do?"

"Why, invite him down for tea, of course!" the captain answered.

"Hear that, boys?" Bill Jukes called from the deck. "Put the kettle on! It's teatime!"

The pirates erupted in cheers and shouts. They knew exactly what "tea" meant to the captain, and headed toward the cannons.

"Tea!" Smee said with delight, not quite picking up on what the captain was implying. "A'ways a good idea."

As Smee disappeared into Hook's quarters to prepare a spot of tea, Bill Jukes approached the captain. He had two large cannonballs under his arm. "Would he like one lump or two?" he asked.

The captain grinned devilishly. "Why not give him all we've got?" he said.

This, he thought as he watched the pirate load the cannon, was going to make the morning much, much better.

CHAPTER FIVE

Wendy still couldn't believe she was in Neverland. Flying through thick, fluffy clouds, she took a deep breath. The air smelled sweeter without the smog of London filling it. And there were no shouts from carriage drivers or people as they tried to push through the crowded streets. Everything was beautiful and peaceful, like something out of a fairy tale....

BOOM!

Wendy cried out as a cannonball ripped through the clouds, narrowly missing her. The shock wave from the blast sent Wendy flying backward, and she spun out of control. Luckily, Peter managed to grab her hand before she could fall.

"What was that?" she asked, breathing heavily.

"Pirates!" Peter answered. "Come on!"

Together, they dove into a massive cloud bank, John and Michael close behind. Above them, another cannonball pierced the air where they had just been. Flying fast, Wendy and Peter broke through the last of the cloud cover and found themselves

right above a large sea stack. Landing on the huge column of rock that towered over the waves below, they looked out at the cove. A ship floated on the water of a tranquil lagoon. The air around it was filled with smoke from cannon fire.

"It's Hook!" Peter said.

John and Michael exchanged nervous glances.

"*Captain* Hook?" John said.

Peter nodded. "Who else would be trying to kill me this early in the morning?"

He said this as though being fired at by huge cannons was something as routine as getting a spot of tea or taking a walk through the park at sunset.

But this was most decidedly *not* routine to the Darlings, and as the cannonballs continued to get closer and closer, the children became more and more nervous. They flew from one sea stack to another, managing to stay just ahead of the cannonballs. Arriving at one of the towers with a ledge that provided some cover, they flew down. As everyone tried to catch their breath and slow their racing hearts, Tink flew up to Peter and chimed as she pointed to the shore.

"Good idea, Tink!" Peter said when she was done.

"What's she saying?" asked Wendy.

"That we should do the sensible thing: we'll take the fight to them!"

Wendy frowned. She looked at Tinker Bell, who was rolling

her eyes. Wendy had the distinct feeling, again, that that was not at all what the fairy had said. But she also got the feeling that Tinker Bell was used to this. Another day, another skirmish. If reality was anything like the stories she knew of Peter and Hook's rivalry, they would always find a way to face off. Peter would toy with Hook, hiding from him and then popping into the open to tease him. Hook would find him and grow angry. Cannonballs would be fired; swords would be drawn. It was—to Peter, at least—like one big game.

Unaware of what Wendy was thinking, Peter got down to business.

"Now listen close," he said to the group. "I'll lead the charge. You three take up the rear. We'll storm them fore to aft." He paused and looked at the *Jolly Roger*. From their vantage point, Peter could see that Hook had brought out the Long Tom. The huge cannon was the longest and most powerful in Hook's artillery. Peter wasn't worried. He went on. "They'll never see us coming! All pirates are fair game, but remember: leave Hook to m—"

BOOM!

The sea stack exploded beneath them, sending all the children flying in different directions. John and Michael clung to each other as the air around them filled with smoke. Wendy tried to keep sight of them, but she had been blasted in the opposite

direction. With her panic growing and her vision clouding, she spiraled toward the sea below.

"Think happy thoughts, think happy thoughts . . ." Wendy chanted over and over, but it didn't help. She was still in a free fall, approaching the water at an alarming rate. No matter what thoughts she tried to think, nothing could get her to fly at that moment.

With a splash, she crashed headlong into the ocean.

The water surrounded her, pulling at her clothes as she struggled to the surface. Bursting above the waves, she coughed and sputtered. She swung her arms, but it was pointless; she couldn't swim with her dress weighed down by water. She was certain she was going to sink below the waves and never surface again. Luckily, the waves were pushing her closer to shore. Going limp, she let them carry her. A short while later, she was washed up onto the rocky beach. As the water receded behind her, the last of her pixie dust faded.

Sitting up, Wendy patted her arms and legs. She couldn't believe she had survived. But then, suddenly, a horrible thought crossed her mind.

"John! Michael! Peter!" she cried out.

No one answered. Her heart began to race as terrible thoughts

filled her mind. Where had they gone? Had they been hurt? Had they been hit by the cannonball? Were they lost and alone and afraid?

As her thoughts spiraled out of control, she looked down at the waves, which continued to wash in and out, and she spotted something in the water below her. Her heart fell as the item became clearer—Peter's hat.

"Oh, no!" she said softly, lifting the hat and holding it gently in her hands.

Looking around, Wendy saw a grassy bluff rising past the seaside. It would give her a better view of the water and surrounding area. She raced toward the bluff and ran up its steep side. By the time she got to the top, she was panting. She scanned the horizon, eager to see any sign of Peter, her brothers, Tink, or even the pirates. But no one was there. The endless sea seemed empty. She was all alone.

Sinking to her knees, Wendy choked back a sob. What was she going to do now? She didn't know where she was, and she couldn't leave Neverland without Tink to give her pixie dust. The adventure suddenly seemed less like a dream and more like a nightmare.

As she sat there, a gust of wind kicked up around her. It rustled through her hair and cooled her flaming cheeks. And then, over the wind, she heard hoofbeats. Turning, Wendy saw a young woman riding up the hill toward her atop the most

magnificent white stallion she had ever seen. As she got closer, Wendy could see that the girl was older than her, but not by much; she was probably fifteen or sixteen. Her dark hair shone in the sun, and her brown eyes were warm as they looked down at Wendy. There was something familiar about the girl, but Wendy couldn't put her finger on it. Had she seen her somewhere before?

Stopping in front of her, the girl began to speak rapidly in a language Wendy did not understand, though she was quite certain that at one point she heard her name.

Finally, the girl stopped and started again. "Are you the Wendy?" she asked in English.

Wendy startled. How did she know her name? *Had* they met? She was still trying to make sense of everything when she saw that the girl was not alone. A group of eight children came up the hill behind her and surrounded the horse. The boys and girls were wearing rags and remnants of school uniforms. A few had on what appeared to be homemade animal costumes like John and Michael wore at Halloween.

"Are you the Wendy?" the girl asked again.

"I'm *a* Wendy," Wendy replied. That seemed a safe enough answer.

One of the children, a tough-looking pale little girl in a rabbit hat and a long brown coat, stepped forward. "The Wendy Peter went to find?"

"The Wendy who knows the bedtime stories?" a little boy around eleven, with brown skin and a purple coat, asked.

Wendy's head turned back and forth between the two. What were they talking about? How did they know any of this? She had the sensation that she knew these children; it was the same sensation she had about the girl.

Just then, twin girls no older than ten, with identical curly dark hair and brown skin, stepped forward. One wore a red coat, and the other blue. Despite their angelic-looking faces, they were all business as they added, "Because if you don't know stories, then you're an impostor."

"And you know what we do with impostors," the girl in the rabbit hat said. To make it clear exactly what they did, she pulled out a dull knife and flashed it in the air.

Wendy immediately put her hands in the air and shook her head. "No! I know stories! Lots of stories!" she said quickly. She didn't like the slightly wild look in the girl's eyes.

"Easy, Curly . . ." the older girl atop the horse said. She dismounted, walked over to Curly, and pushed down Curly's knife. The tension eased, and in that moment, Wendy realized exactly why she thought she knew the older girl.

"Are you . . . Tiger Lily?" she asked.

"You know my name?" the girl said.

It was all beginning to make sense. If she was Tiger Lily, a girl

who belonged to the native tribe of Neverland and often helped Peter in the stories Wendy had heard in the nursery . . .

Wendy turned and looked around at the children. "Which means that you must be . . ."

"Lost Boys," one of them, a peach-skinned boy, finished. He was older than the others, closer to thirteen, and wore a green jacket and a brown triangular hat. "Every last one of us."

Wendy looked at the group and thought of all the stories she had heard about these very children. Now they were standing right in front of her, as alive as Peter. She went through them, mentally matching the children in front of her with the descriptions from the stories. There was Curly, whose toughness Wendy now remembered. Slightly was the one who had just spoken. And then there was Tootles, the one in the purple coat. But while the names were familiar, there was something that didn't quite add up.

"You're not all boys," she pointed out.

"So?" said one of the twins, a hand on her hip.

"I guess . . . I guess it doesn't matter," Wendy said. In the stories she knew, the Lost Boys had always been, well, boys. This was definitely different. Just like everything was proving to be about the real Neverland.

Another girl stepped forward. This, Wendy assumed from her coat made of leaves and her short black hair in pigtails, was

Birdie. "What matters," she said, "is what you've done with Peter."

Wendy shook her head. "I didn't *do* anything with Peter," she protested. "He's the one who brought me here. Me and my brothers . . ."

"Brothers!"

Wendy looked down at the surprised cry that came from near her feet. A smaller boy, wearing glasses and a fox costume, looked up at her, and she realized he'd been tying her shoelaces together. She bit back a smile. This had to be Nibs. He was always described as a trickster of sorts. And he reminded her of John and Michael.

"Peter didn't say anything about brothers," the twins said in unison.

Wendy was surprised by how upset the Lost Boys seemed at the news that it wasn't just her. But she pressed on. "Well, that's what I'm trying to tell you! *We* were flying along when we were attacked!"

Curly raised an eyebrow. "Attacked?"

Wendy nodded. "By pirates! They shot at us!" As if it might prove a point, Wendy held up Peter's hat.

A few of the Lost Boys let out shouts, another couple sniffled, and the rest lowered their heads. They were quite used to Peter flying off and fighting Hook. But it was rare that he seemed to be in actual danger.

"I knew it!" Tootles cried as he rubbed his nose. "I knew this was a bad day to fly."

Slightly shot him a look. Before they started making assumptions about anything, it was best to see what was really going on. "Telescope!"

He took a telescope from the last Lost Boy, aged twelve or so, whose face was partially covered by a wooden mask. Wendy frowned, thinking through the stories. Who was this older boy with the dark hair? *Bellweather!* The name came to her in a flash. Focusing, she watched Slightly run to the edge of the bluff, hold up the telescope, which was really nothing more than a hollow piece of driftwood, and look out.

"These brothers of yours . . ." Slightly said as he moved the telescope back and forth. "What do they look like?"

"They're . . . well, they're *this* tall," Wendy said, holding her hand by her hip to indicate Michael's height. "And *this* tall," she said, reaching her hand to her shoulder for John's. She also pointed out that John had a hat and Michael a bear.

"A *real* bear?" Tootles asked, looking excited.

Grabbing the telescope from Slightly, Curly scanned the skies. "It's pirates, all right," she said. She passed the telescope to Wendy.

"I can't see anything," Wendy said as she held the driftwood to her eye.

She heard several of the Lost Boys murmur something about

her being too grown-up. But she ignored them. It wasn't her fault. The driftwood was *not* a telescope.

Nibs tugged at her sleeve. "Yes, you can. You're just looking the wrong way," he said gently. He nodded at the driftwood, encouraging her to try again.

Taking a deep breath, Wendy lifted it once more to her eye. Only this time, she tried to see what all the Lost Boys saw—something, anything. To her surprise, it worked. At the other end of the hollow driftwood, images began to appear.

"I see it!" she said. "I see a pirate ship and . . . pirates and . . ." Her voice caught in her throat.

There, being lifted out of a dinghy and onto the deck of the *Jolly Roger*, were John and Michael. They had been caught!

CHAPTER
SIX

"**C**ome along, lads," Smee said over his shoulder as he led John and Michael across the deck of the *Jolly Roger*.

The boys were looking around, both fear and wonder on their faces, though there was definitely more fear than wonder in Michael's expression. Smee felt a bit bad. He didn't like to see little ones upset. But he *really* didn't like to see Hook upset. And when he walked into the cabin with these two, the captain would be pleased.

But first they had to stop dragging their feet. Hoping a kind word might move them along, he went on. "Don't fancy yourself the first half-pints to be found afloatin'. Why, I rescued the cap'n from the sea when he was scarcely taller than yourselves."

The other pirates, having helped Smee and the boys onto the deck, now formed a maze for them to get through. The grubby men and women shouted and booed and cheered, some happy to have a prize, others annoyed by the boys' presence.

"That's a fine bear you got there!" one of them said as Michael passed by. "You kill that yourself?"

Michael looked horrified and pulled Mr. Bear closer to his chest. "Don't you touch Mr. Bear!" he shouted.

Just then, they arrived in front of the captain's cabin. A new door was in the process of being hung on the doorframe. Smee looked at the boys, and then, clearing his throat, he entered. The boys followed.

Captain Hook sat writing a letter at his desk in his dark cabin. On his prized phonograph, an opera played, almost making the gloomy space seem brighter. Almost. The little light that did make its way into the quarters was weak and revealed air full of smoke and incense. Hearing a commotion at the door, Hook looked up to see Smee pushing two young boys into the room.

"What news do you bring me, Mr. Smee?" he asked. "Good tidings, I hope?"

Smee, mishearing the man, as usual, replied, "Well, the tide is out, Captain, as is customary at this time of day, but—"

"News, Mr. Smee," Hook interrupted. "News. Did we hit the boy?"

Ever since their little "tea party" earlier, Hook had been waiting anxiously for word on his nemesis. It was frightfully aggravating to have to wait so long. To Hook's further aggravation, Mr. Smee shook his head.

"Oh! No, no, not today," Smee said. "But we fished *these* little

fellas out o' the drink, one of whom is in possession of a small but possibly dangerous bear. . . ."

Upon hearing this, Michael and John, who had been keeping their heads down, looked at each other. Did these pirates really think Mr. Bear was dangerous? What sort of pirates believed a stuffed animal could do anything more than be cuddled?

Mr. Smee continued, pointing out that perhaps the boys were compatriots of a certain flying nuisance. But Hook was no longer listening—at least not to Smee. Reaching over, he stopped the record on his phonograph with an ear-piercing screech. Then he stood up. Looming over the terrified boys, he took John's chin in his hand.

"Listen," he said. "Do you hear what I hear?"

John shook his head. "I don't think so . . ." he said nervously.

Hook, with his eyes now wide and panicked, shook his head. "Shhh!" he said, his own *shhh* louder than John's answer had been. "There it is again. A teeny, tiny . . ."

His voice trailed off as the panic in his eyes increased. Hook could hear it. The tiny *tick, tick, tick*. It was filling him with dread, filling him with fear. And he hated those feelings. Lashing out suddenly, he ripped through the pocket of John's pajamas with his hook. When he pulled his hook free, John's pocket watch dangled from the end. Hook stared at it as though it might bite.

"Smee!" he called.

"Yes, Cap'n?"

Hook whipped around, the pocket watch swinging wildly. "What are the rules on my ship?"

Smee put a finger in the air. "As they be tattooed on my heart!" he began. "One: each pirate upon their first embarking shall be entitled at journey's end to two and three-fifths of a share of all—"

Hook stopped him. "No, no. Start at rule thirty-seven."

Smee nodded. "Ah, yes," he said. "Quite right. Rule thirty-seven: no one shall say the boy's name. Rule thirty-eight: no whistling. And rule thirty-nine is . . ." Smee struggled to remember.

Hook had no trouble reminding him. Taking John's pocket watch and smashing it on the ground, he snarled the last rule. "No! Clocks!"

After making sure that the timepiece was well and truly crushed, Hook once again looked at the boys.

"Now, how did you come here? To Neverland?" he asked.

"We came with—" Michael started, but he was quickly stopped by Smee.

"Remember the rules!" Smee whispered. "Don't say his name!"

"We don't care about your rules!" John said, stamping his foot. He was quite upset about the loss of his watch and so was not as reserved as usual. "We came here with Peter Pan!"

Michael nodded. "And he's going to rescue us!"

From outside where the door to the cabin *should have* been came a gasp. The pirates had heard John say Peter's name. "Dibs on the bear after he executes them," one of them said.

Ignoring the eavesdropping crew, Hook stared at the boys in front of him. Then a steely glint settled in his eyes as a plan came to him. "He's going to rescue you, is he?"

John gulped. Hate was radiating from Hook. Hate and something much more dangerous. Whatever the man was planning, it wasn't going to be good—for them or Peter. Perhaps he and his brother should have stayed quiet. "Well . . . probably?" he said, trying to backpedal.

"Hopefully," Michael added.

A smile, or more of a sneer, spread across Hook's face. Most days, the word *hope* made him ill. But not today. Today it gave him a wonderful idea—a way to rid himself of these two and, even better, rid himself of Peter Pan once and for all. "Are you thinking what I'm thinking, Mr. Smee?"

Outside the cabin, the gathered pirates began to mumble excitedly. They knew exactly what he was thinking. "He's gonna make them walk the plank . . ." Scrimshaw Sam said, his eyes holding far too much glee for such a serious statement.

Inside, Smee had an entirely different idea of what the captain had in mind. "That a cuppa tea would be nice?" he said. Hook frowned at him, and Smee tried again. "That we should look upon this rare opportunity to take the high road in life, to let boys

be boys and curs be curs and go our separate ways with no harm done?" Hook's frown deepened, and Smee sighed. "Or we could make them walk the plank."

Hook stood up. "It *is* a fine day for a planking, but I've got a better idea." Walking out onto the deck, he looked at his crew. "Rouse yourselves, lads," he ordered. "And set a course for Skull Rock."

Wendy, Tiger Lily, and the Lost Boys stood atop a cliff of bright red rock. Through the telescope, Curly was tracking the pirates' every move. And she didn't like what she was seeing.

"Skull Rock," she said, watching as the sails on the *Jolly Roger* unfurled and the ship began to sail out of the lagoon and toward a towering mass of land that looked exactly as its name suggested. "Just as I feared."

She handed the telescope back to Wendy, who looked through it once more. "Oh, my . . ."

Silently, the group began to make their way down the red rocks toward the lower ground. Bellweather helped the smallest, while the older children carefully maneuvered the rocks.

"There's only one reason pirates go to Skull Rock," Tiger Lily said when they were closer.

Curly nodded, her face grim. "An execution is nigh."

Wendy didn't need to hear more. There was no way she was

letting her brothers get executed. "Well, what are we waiting for? Let's go rescue them!"

This didn't sit well with some of the Lost Boys. "But what's a rescue without Peter Pan?" Nibs asked softly.

Walking over and giving the young boy a slap on his back, Slightly smiled. "And what's a Peter Pan without his Lost Boys? Chin up, Nibs."

Nodding, Tiger Lily pointed ahead. "This way!" she said. "Shortcut!"

As the others followed Tiger Lily toward a nearby tunnel, Wendy took a peek back at Skull Rock. The *Jolly Roger* had anchored, and she could just make out four small dinghies being lowered toward the water. On one of those boats were her brothers. And she was going to rescue them—Peter Pan or no Peter Pan.

Turning, she ran after the group and joined them just as they walked into the tunnel. It was dark and smelled like damp earth. Tiger Lily struck a flint against the rocky sides and lit her torch. As the flame pushed away the dark, Wendy gasped. They were inside a huge cavernous space. The walls were made of rough rock, and the ground was packed dirt. A path led through the middle of it.

"You can get anywhere in Neverland down here," Tiger Lily said as she moved forward in the tunnel, "if you know the way."

As Wendy's eyes adjusted to the flickering light, she saw that the rock walls were not the plain ones she would have expected. They were, in fact, covered in paintings. She stepped closer and saw that many of them depicted a woman on horseback leading a group of warriors. The woman looked familiar.

"Tiger Lily," Wendy said, turning to the girl, "is that you?"

Tiger Lily shook her head. "No. That is my great-great-grandmother. The leader of my tribe. She's the one who led us to Neverland . . ."

"And when Hook and his pirates first laid siege, she brought everyone down here to stay safe," Curly said, bouncing on her toes as she told the tale she had clearly heard many times before.

Nibs nodded. "Those were terrible times," he said, sounding more like a wise old man than a little boy.

"Until we fought back," Tiger Lily said.

Wendy stared at the paintings, trying to imagine what it must have been like for Tiger Lily's people, to be in this new place, under attack. She imagined they had felt a lot like she did at this very moment. Scared, but determined. There was no way she would let Hook hurt her brothers, just like Tiger Lily's ancestors wouldn't let him hurt them. She sighed.

"Oh, why is Captain Hook so hateful?" she asked. Wendy's question had all the Lost Boys eager to talk. One by one, they filled in the rest of the tale.

"Because he grew up," Tootles said.

"And grew up wrong," the twins added.

Birdie nodded. "But he's still the best swordsman."

"Which also makes him the worst," added the twins.

"Which is why we leave him to Peter," Curly pointed out.

Slightly jumped in. "Who he hates, because Peter cut off his hand . . ."

"In a duel," Nibs concluded. "And . . ."

"And fed it to a crocodile?" Wendy asked, remembering this part of the story from when her mother told it. "Along with his watch?"

Surprised, Tootles cocked his head. "You know about the crocodile?"

"That is how the story goes, isn't it?" she replied.

Nibs clapped his hands, and the rest of the group exchanged happy looks. "Peter was right!" he said. "You do know stories! Can you tell us one now?"

Wendy smiled. It was sweet of Nibs to want to hear a story. "Like what?"

"Shhh!" Tiger Lily interjected, holding a finger to her mouth.

They waited for a moment, unsure why they were being quiet or what Tiger Lily was listening for. And then they heard it: the unmistakable sound of pirates singing.

They were getting close.

CHAPTER
SEVEN

Wendy and the others emerged from the tunnel onto a ledge that overlooked the whole inside of Skull Rock. It was more terrible than she ever could have imagined. Magma had formed the cavern thousands of years earlier, and numerous volcanic glowing red stalactites and stalagmites pointed down and up. They looked like the horrible teeth of a fearsome monster, about to devour its prey. Ancient stone steps had been carved into the rocks, leading down to the water and a grotto. The grotto was filled with water that came in from the outside, rising and falling with the tide. Right then, the tide was out, and a large flat rock, almost resembling an altar, was visible at the grotto's center. Chains dangled from the top of it, and as Wendy peered closer, she saw skeletons: the remains of those poor souls who had come to the altar—and never left.

Dragging her eyes from the rock, Wendy realized with a shudder that if she didn't do something, her brothers could be in big trouble.

"There they are!" she cried, spotting John and Michael. The

pirates were dragging them from one of the dinghies to the rock. As several pirates chained them up, Wendy shivered in fear. "Oh, for goodness' sake, Michael doesn't even know how to swim!"

"We're outnumbered," Tiger Lily said, not helping Wendy's growing fear.

Slightly nodded. "As usual."

Wendy looked back and forth between her brothers and the Lost Boys. The Lost Boys seemed far too calm. Why were they just standing there?

"So what's the plan, then?" she asked.

"Simple," Curly said. "We wait for the pirates to leave. . . ."

"Tide'll be in before that happens," Birdie pointed out.

Tootles shrugged. "Surely they can handle a *little* drowning."

"No!" Wendy sobbed. "No drowning!" They had to have a better plan than that.

But what, she wondered, was it? And where was Peter?

Hook watched as his crew chained John and Michael to the rock. He smiled. He really did love when a plan came together. And this one was coming together beautifully. They had even managed to chain up the smaller boy's precious bear. Soon Peter would have no choice but to show up and rescue these poor, helpless children. Then the fight could commence.

But first there was no harm having a little fun with them.

"Tide's rising, my little castaways," he said. "What will you hold on to—your hope, or your breath?"

He cast a quick look around. The line was quite brilliant, if he did say so himself. It would be the perfect time for Peter to swoop in. When he didn't, Hook turned his attention back to the boys.

The older one, John, was struggling against the chains. "You can't kill us! We haven't done anything wrong!"

Hook shook his head. "Oh, but you have," he said most seriously. "We've caught you in the act of being a child, and we can't have children in Neverland!"

"Rule number forty-four: no children in Neverland!" Smee declared, happy to support his captain.

Around them the other pirates nodded and shouted in agreement.

"No children in Neverland!" Bill Jukes repeated.

"No children in Neverland!" Scrimshaw Sam shouted.

One by one, the others echoed the mantra, shouting until the rock around them seemed to shake. Caught up in the moment, they howled as another gangly pirate with a long beard let out his own shout: "No one but children in Neverland!"

Not realizing the rule had been inverted, the other pirates began to chant this instead.

Realizing what had happened, Hook shouted angrily, which silenced them.

Slowly, he stared daggers into each and every one of his crew

members, trying to figure out who was behind the taunt. When he spotted the gangly pirate, his eyes narrowed. "You there," he shouted. "How long have you sailed on my ship?"

Approaching the pirate as he spoke, Hook was able to get a better look at him. He was certainly an odd-looking fellow. He wore an eye patch and a copper nose, and his beard was particularly large. If he had been on the ship long, Hook would have remembered.

Just then Bill Jukes reached out and gave the gangly pirate's beard a yank. It came off, revealing none other than Peter Pan.

Smee cocked his head, not realizing what was going on. "What's he have that on for?"

But Hook wasn't confused. He was furious. His eyes widened as he whispered fiercely, "Pan!"

As the rest of the crew gasped, Peter shrugged. "Have to say, it's not half bad being a pirate!"

Bill Jukes, none too pleased to have been fooled along with the rest of them, swung his arm back and punched at Peter. Lightning-quick, Peter ducked, while the hat he had been wearing—with Tinker Bell hidden inside—floated upward, trailing pixie dust. Jukes looked at the spot where Peter should have been, and saw him clambering out of his disguise.

"But it's far better being me!" Peter said, finishing his thought.

And just like that, the scene exploded with noise. Pirates roared at the tops of their lungs and rushed toward Peter, swords

swinging. With practiced ease, Peter ducked under an oncoming pirate, causing him to crash into another. He barely used the sword in his hand, instead leaping about like a merry prankster as the bumbling pirates tried—and failed—to get to him. Tinker Bell joined in the fray, flashing like a firefly and distracting the pirates with her brilliant glow. As some chased her, Peter gave chase to others. While the scene appeared tense, Peter had a smile on his face as he knocked over pirates one by one.

Jumping past one pirate, Peter suddenly found himself face to face with the pointed end of Bill Jukes's harpoon. Not stopping, Peter leapt onto it and ran down the length of the large weapon. He hopped onto Jukes's shoulders and pulled the big pirate to the ground. Peter laughed. This was too easy.

Just then, out of the corner of his eye he saw a sword aimed at him slice through the air. Missing him, it hit Michael's bear, cutting one of the stuffed animal's arms clean off.

"No!" Michael cried as he watched the bear's arm fall off the rock and into the water below.

Peter turned, his energy renewed after seeing a helpless bear harmed, and took care of the last of the pirates. Twirling his sword, he looked around, pleased. Beside him, Tinker Bell yawned, as if this was just something the two of them did for fun.

But there was one more person to fight: Hook. The pirate stood on his boat, looking across the short distance to where

The Darling children love pretending to be their storybook hero, Peter Pan, and his nemesis, Captain Hook.

But one night, the fun and games lead to a shattered mirror in the nursery.

Mr. Darling scolds the children—especially Wendy, the eldest, who should know better.

Wendy is supposed to leave home tomorrow for school, but she tells her mother she isn't sure she's ready to grow up.

Peter Pan and Tinker Bell hear Wendy's wish and whisk the children to Neverland! An attack by Captain Hook separates Wendy from the others, but she finds a friend in the brave Tiger Lily.

Alongside Tiger Lily, Wendy meets the Lost Boys, loyal
friends to Peter Pan.

The group heads to Skull Rock to save Wendy's brothers
from Hook. Fortunately, Tiger Lily knows a shortcut through
the caves.

Peter Pan appears to duel with Hook! The children safely escape and head to Peter and the Lost Boys' hideout.

The Lost Boys miss the families they can't remember, and Wendy comforts them with a lullaby. Hook hears Wendy's song from afar . . . and follows the sound.

A downtrodden Peter finally confides in Wendy: he and Hook used to be friends! Then Hook finds the hideout—and shockingly, defeats Peter in a duel.

Hook captures the children, and Wendy steps up to become a leader! Peter reappears, and after they work together to foil Hook, he flies the children safely home to London.

Peter stood atop a rock. For a moment, the enemies just stood there, locked in an age-old battle.

"Captain Hook!" Peter said, as if he had not just single-handedly put the man's crew in their place. "You're looking a little worse for wear, old man. Are you sure you wouldn't be happier back in your sickbed?"

Hook shook his head. "Not today, boy," he said. "I woke up this morning with a song in my heart. And do you know what the refrain was?" He waited for Peter to answer, but the boy just shrugged. *"Today Peter Pan shall perish!"* he sang out.

Peter did not seem impressed. He had heard it all before. And the talk was boring. It was time for action. "Dark and sinister man," he said, "prepare to meet thy doom!"

"Proud and insolent youth," Hook countered, "have at me!"

Both pirate and boy drew their swords, and then, in a movement that appeared as choreographed and well-rehearsed as a dance number, they leapt into the air. Their swords plunged down and met with a clang and a flash of sparks, making a metal X between the two of them.

The duel was on.

CHAPTER EIGHT

Standing on the ledge that looked over Skull Rock's cove, Wendy fumed. She was sick of this. She and the others had watched the whole thing unfold. And at first she had cheered with the rest of the Lost Boys as Peter appeared and began to take down the pirates. But when he had done nothing to help Michael—or his poor wounded bear—Wendy finally stopped enjoying the show and got fed up instead.

"Why won't he rescue them?" she asked, nodding at her brothers. The water had begun to rise, and she gulped nervously. They were in danger! "He can fight Hook later!"

"He could," the twins answered together. Then they shrugged. "But he won't."

Curly nodded in agreement. "Hook always comes first."

Stepping forward, Tiger Lily placed a hand on Wendy's shoulder. Wendy turned and their eyes met, flashing with understanding.

"Follow me," Tiger Lily said.

Wendy's eyes darted back and forth between Peter and her

brothers. Peter was leading Hook all over the place, seemingly oblivious to the real danger her brothers faced. She frowned as she heard the pair trading jabs.

"Here is the story of your downfall, boy," Hook said. "You may never grow older, but neither shall you ever get stronger."

Peter laughed. "I'm happy to be less strong if it means I shan't be so sad a fellow as you. Do you cry yourself to sleep at night, waiting for that *ticktock, ticktock* to stop?"

Wendy shook her head. Peter could pretend this was all a game, but she needed to save her brothers. Taking a breath, Wendy followed Tiger Lily down the rock face toward the duelers. The sides of the rock were sheer and treacherous. Wendy moved carefully and slowly, imitating Tiger Lily's more practiced movements. Hand over hand, inch by inch, they made their way down.

Finally reaching the bottom, Wendy let out a shaky sigh. A part of her wanted to sink to the ground and take a break. But Tiger Lily was already jumping from one rock to the next, her gaze focused on Michael and John. Wendy took a deep breath and followed.

At first, the distance between the rocks and the crashing waves below slowed Wendy down. But seeing her brothers' frightened faces and the steadily rising water spurred her on. Pretending she was playing a game of hopscotch, Wendy moved faster, catching up to Tiger Lily. When they reached the outcropping in the center, Wendy sighed in relief. They had made it. Now they just needed to save her brothers.

"John! Michael!" Wendy rushed to the boys and tried to give them a hug. Unfortunately, they were both now nearly chest deep in water.

"Wendy!" they said, clearly happy to see her.

"Look what they did to Mr. Bear!" Michael added, holding up his maimed teddy.

Wendy gave him a sympathetic frown but then put her finger to her lips. They couldn't afford to draw any attention to themselves. While Wendy kept her brothers calm, Tiger Lily tried to cut the chains. But it was no use. They were thick and rusty with age.

Hearing a familiar chime, Wendy looked up. "Tinker Bell!"

Somehow, the little creature had heard Tiger Lily and raced away from Peter to see what was going on.

"Can you help us?"

Tinker Bell chimed a clear yes.

Wendy sighed with relief as the fairy assessed the situation. She flew around the boys, peering closely at the chains. Then, spotting the lock, she smiled. Reaching into the keyhole with her tiny hand, she shook her arm. The lock filled with pixie dust. As soon as the whole thing was glowing gold, Tinker Bell gritted her teeth and leaned into the lock. Slowly, it began to buckle, and then, with a loud *pop*, it snapped open. The boys—and the bear—were free!

"Yes!" Wendy shouted, forgetting her own rule to be quiet.

Hearing her shout, Peter finally noticed Wendy and Tiger Lily.

"Wendy!" he called. "You're still alive!"

Unfortunately, Wendy didn't have time to point out that she had, in fact, been alive all this time and Peter simply hadn't noticed because he was too caught up in his fight. Because at that moment, Hook grabbed Peter's shadow while he was distracted, and gave it a hard yank. Peter fell to the ground. Before Peter could scurry away, the captain raised his foot high and brought it down, pinning Peter to the rocky bank.

"Ha!" he shouted with glee. "I got you! I beat you!" Tinker Bell rushed to help Peter, but when Hook pressed a blade against Peter's throat, she stopped in midair. "Don't even think about it, fairy."

"Very bad form, Captain Hook," Peter said, his voice calm despite the sword at his throat.

Hook laughed. "All my bad form I learnt from thee," he retorted.

"Ah, don't flatter yourself," Peter said. "You've always been rotten. A stinking, rotten . . . codfish."

For just the briefest of flashes, Hook looked like a little boy with hurt feelings. Watching from a safe distance, Wendy saw that flash. How many times had they had this conversation? she wondered. How many times had Peter said the same words?

Before she could wonder more, the look disappeared and his usual scowl returned.

"You have stabbed me in the heart with your words for the last time," said Hook. "At last, I shall return in kind with my sword."

Hook lifted his blade.

"Strike, then," Peter said, his expression brave. "If you've got the courage, and strike true. For to die . . ."

"Would be an awfully big adventure," Hook finished, pulling the sword back.

Wendy's eyes narrowed. Had she been right? Hook had known exactly what Peter was going to say.

"Stop!" she shouted.

Her voice echoed off the cave walls, making it sound as if a hundred Wendys had called for a stop. It worked. Hook lowered his sword slightly and turned his gaze on Wendy. He squinted.

"Who are you?" he asked. "I've not seen you before."

Wendy gulped. She hadn't been thinking clearly when she shouted. She just hadn't wanted to see Peter get hurt. But now all eyes were on her. "I . . . well . . . you see, I . . ."

"She's a Wendy!" Curly finished for her, calling down from the ledge.

Hook looked confused. "Wendy? What's a Wendy?"

"*I'm* a Wendy," she said, Curly's words giving her courage. "Wendy Moira Angela Darling, and I'm from London, England, where gentlemen do not harm children."

Hook scoffed. "Well, I am—"

"Captain Hook," Wendy finished for him, not sounding impressed. "I know."

"And we are in—"

"Neverland," Wendy said, again stopping Hook from finishing.

Getting frustrated, Hook forged on, this time speaking swiftly, so as not to be interrupted. "And . . . this child is not a child. Nor I a gentleman. So say your goodbyes, for you shan't see him in this world ag—"

Before Hook could finish, a very loud *tick* interrupted him.

Hook's eyes flashed. His nostrils flared.

TOCK!

Now Hook's eyes dropped to the ground nervously. The ticking, the tocking. The noises were coming from beneath the very rock he stood on—the very rock on which he had Peter pinned.

TICK! TOCK!

Anxiously, he tapped his foot on the ground. To his horror, the ground trembled. As Hook and everyone else watched, the rock lifted from the water, revealing it was not a rock at all, but a monstrous spiny, barnacle-laden crocodile. Hook was lifted with the creature, perched precariously on his head.

"Whoa," John breathed.

"That is one big . . ." Michael started.

The crocodile opened his massive jaws. Hook's legs, one on

each part of the creature's mouth, began to spread apart. The ticking grew louder, coming from deep inside the crocodile's gut. Hook's face had gone white at both the sound and his situation.

Just when it looked like Hook might meet his end, one of his crew, Scrimshaw Sam, appeared on a nearby rock. Harpoon in hand, he lunged at the creature. The crocodile did not seem fazed by either Sam's loud shouts or his weapon. Tossing Hook aside, the creature whirled around and, with a flick of his mighty tail, sent the newly arrived pirate flying across the cave. As the pirate shouted in fright, the crocodile lunged and, in a single bite, devoured him.

As the other pirates began to panic, Hook clambered up onto the cave wall. Looking over his shoulder, he saw that the crocodile, with his appetizer finished, had turned and was coming back toward him. Then Smee waved at him from the front of the tunnel, and he hightailed it that way.

Seeing his own chance to escape, Peter leapt onto the rock with the Darlings and Tiger Lily.

"Come on!" he said. "Grab hands."

As soon as they were linked together, Peter took off into the air, pulling them all with him, up, up . . . and out a hole at the very top of Skull Rock, passing the Lost Boys rushing up the outer path.

They were all safe.

For now.

So was Hook, who had managed to narrowly escape the crocodile's jaws. He made it to Smee and kept running. All around him, the other pirates fled, too. Some ran; some swam. The sounds of the crocodile's thrashing tail and chomping teeth echoed through the cavern. Spotting a dinghy outside the entrance to Skull Rock, Hook didn't hesitate. Arms flailing and legs kicking, he leapt—and landed in the water with a splash right beside the dinghy. He pulled himself in and started to paddle away even as Smee jumped into the boat. The crocodile kept chasing them. But before the creature could snatch up his prey, Hook and Smee snuck through a thin opening in the rock face. The crocodile, too big to fit through, was left to snap at them angrily.

Standing atop Skull Rock, Peter stared down at his nemesis. Wendy, her eyes fixed on Peter, shook her head. There was something boastful in his look. And frankly, she wasn't sure he deserved to be quite so pleased with himself.

Peter turned and looked at the rest of them. "Well, that was fun!"

Wendy couldn't help herself: she slapped him—hard—across the face. *Fun?* Was risking her brothers' lives fun? Was facing swords and killer crocodiles a good time? She most certainly thought not. Shaking her head, she turned and followed Tiger Lily as the girl led them off the rock.

Behind her, Peter frowned, putting a hand to his stinging cheek.

CHAPTER NINE

Peter's hand was still on his cheek a short time later. The group had made it off Skull Rock and reconnected with the Lost Boys and Tiger Lily's horse, and now they journeyed through grassy highlands. The farther they got from the shore and the terrible cave, the softer everything became. Everything, that is, except Wendy. She was still sore at Peter, and they continued to argue the whole way.

"It was an *adventure*!" Peter said. "Isn't that what you wanted?"

Wendy clenched her hands into fists. "Yes! But I didn't think that meant being shot out of the sky by pirates . . ."

"Or drowned," John added.

"Or dismembered," Michael said, holding up his teddy. The little bear was most certainly worse for wear.

Peter looked among them all, and then he shrugged. He didn't seem to know what to say, which was even more infuriating to Wendy. She let out a harrumph. At the same time, Tinker Bell chimed.

Wendy sighed in frustration. "Oh, Tink, what are you saying?"

"What she's saying is I saved the day," Peter said, happy to translate.

Tinker Bell raised an eyebrow, looking surprised. Then she chimed something else.

But Peter and Wendy had already moved on.

"You *sort of* saved the day," Wendy said, with her arms now crossed over her chest and her chin in the air. She wasn't about to back down. "You saved *part* of the day."

Peter nodded, missing the dig. "And I did a pretty good job at it."

"Clearly," Wendy said with a roll of her eyes. "It's not like you had any help."

"I didn't," Peter said. "I'm Peter Pan. I don't ever need help."

Wendy threw her hands into the air. Did he truly not see that he'd had help—loads of it? From Tiger Lily to the Lost Boys to Tinker Bell. "You have a magical fairy who makes you fly. Do you really think you could beat Captain Hook on your own?"

Peter looked offended—and a bit surprised. He was obviously not used to anyone calling him out. "I always beat him. That's just how it works. Always has, always will."

"And what happens if it doesn't?" Tiger Lily asked from atop her huge stallion, raising the question that had been on the tip of Wendy's tongue. Peter shot her an angry look. But Tiger Lily just shrugged. Her question landed hard on the Lost Boys, who looked at each other in shock and then at Peter.

"That won't ever happen, will it, Peter?" Nibs asked nervously.

Peter hesitated, and Wendy wondered if perhaps the question had gotten to him. But then he waved a hand in the air.

"Of course not," he said. "Nothing ever changes in Neverland. Least of all me."

Peter leapt into the air, flew ahead, and quickly disappeared from sight. Tinker Bell lingered, looking between Peter and Wendy, but then she, too, followed, a trail of pixie dust in her wake.

Wendy sighed. She hadn't meant to upset Peter. But he was the leader. He should take responsibility for what he did—and didn't—do. She resumed her walk through the tall grass until Tootles's voice, right beside her, startled her.

"It's not true what Peter said, you know," he said, his voice soft. His eyes darted back and forth as if he was nervous about speaking. "Some things do change."

"Shhh!" Slightly hissed.

"You're not supposed to talk about that," the twins added.

Confused, Wendy looked at the Lost Boys. "What shouldn't we talk about?"

None of the children answered. Instead, they all ran ahead, eager to get away from the forbidden topic. All, that is, except Curly.

Standing up on her tiptoes, Curly whispered into Wendy's ear, "Hook wasn't always Hook."

And then, before Wendy could begin to make sense of that, Curly raced off, leaving Wendy alone. *What does that mean?* she wondered as she slowly followed. And how would she ever find out?

Captain Hook was not pleased. In fact, as he crawled onto the shore after his narrow escape from the jaws of the hand-eating crocodile, he was exhausted and full of rage.

Around him, the other pirates who had escaped from Skull Rock were struggling to their feet. They were waterlogged, their hair drenched and their eyes red from the salt water, but they had survived—which was more than could be said about some of the crew. Spitting out a stream of water, Bill Jukes watched as fellow pirate Gurley fastened Mr. Bear's arm onto a necklace and hung it around his neck.

Ignoring the others, Hook sneered. "Never again, Mr. Smee!" he said as he struggled to stand in the thick sand. "Never again shall I be so humiliated."

"A familiar refrain," Mr. Smee said as he wrung out his belt.

Hook's eyes narrowed, but he ignored his first mate. He held up his hook. "My hook is rusting away!" he cried.

"It's just a little wet is all," Smee said, trying to comfort the agitated captain.

But Hook was not having it. Even the suggestion of a rest was tossed aside. Hook wanted nothing but to get back to his ship. But then he remembered the crocodile. He was out there somewhere, just waiting for his chance to pounce.

When Hook said as much to Smee, the older man shook his head. "Remains at large, sir," he said.

Smee gestured to the water lapping at their feet. No crocodile. No ticking. No tocking. It was all quiet.

"Like the boy," Hook said when he saw Smee was right. "Today started off so well."

Smee shrugged. The good-natured soul was always trying to see the best of a situation. He was quite the opposite of his captain.

"There's always tomorrow, sir," Smee suggested.

Hook shook his head. "No!" he shouted, scaring the other pirates, who were still trying to catch their breath and get water out of their boots. "No more tomorrows. Tonight! We will return to the ship . . ."

"Perhaps, Captain," Smee said, raising a finger. "If I may suggest . . ."

But Hook brushed him off. He was focused on his new plan. "We shall prepare to attack . . ."

"The boy . . . he lives on land," Smee added.

Hook nodded and rolled his eyes. Of course the boy lived on land. He knew that. What kind of imbecile did Smee take him for? His brilliant plan was to attack when Peter took flight in the morning.

"*Land,*" Smee repeated, not giving up, "which is where we currently find ourselves."

Hook paused mid-planning. He looked at his feet, which were, undeniably, on land. It was wet, but it was land. He looked back up at Smee and narrowed his eyes. "Go on."

The man gulped nervously. He was not used to people actually listening to him. Fidgeting with his belt, he tried to say out loud what had been racing through his head. "Well, it's like this. I think to myself, standing on solid ground as we currently find ourselves: where on land might the boy be?" As he continued, he grew bolder and his words came faster. "And then I say, well, I don't know myself, but I'd wager there's one person who might know where on this island he resides. One who might *remember* . . ."

"Who?" Hook asked eagerly, forgetting for a moment to be the stern pirate captain he was known to be.

Smee stopped playing with his belt. He peered up at the captain over his spectacles as if waiting for the man to figure it out himself. But Hook just looked blankly back at him. Finally, Smee spoke. "Why, you, sir. *You.*"

Hook's head snapped up. And slowly, ever so slowly, the wheels began to turn. Perhaps Smee was on to something. Maybe there was a way he could find the boy and put an end to this game once and for all.

CHAPTER TEN

Tinker Bell led the group through the thick forest, her sparkling pixie dust lighting the way. The Lost Boys formed a line behind her, followed by John and Michael. Wendy brought up the rear, keeping a keen eye on her brothers. While her steps were nervous and unsure, the Lost Boys tromped ahead, clearly familiar with the unseen path through the trees.

The path came to an abrupt end at a stone wall covered in moss and weathered a deep dark gray. It looked to have been there for hundreds of years. And right where the path ended was a narrow doorway that had been carved into the middle of the wall. Its dark wood warped and rough, the doorway was as ancient-looking as the wall itself.

"What is this place?" John asked. It was the same question Wendy had been asking herself.

"It's home," Curly replied.

All three Darling children tilted their heads back and looked up. In the darkness, they could barely make out the silhouette of a large manor just beyond the wall. Even in the dim light, Wendy

could tell that it was an impressive structure. More castle than house, it had a huge stone tower that reached up to the tips of the tree branches.

"*This* is where you live?" John asked.

Slightly shrugged. "When we feel like it," he answered.

Eyes wide, Wendy started to follow the group through the door when she noticed that Tiger Lily was hanging back. The girl's expression was hard to read in the darkening shadows. Only her white horse could be clearly seen.

"Aren't you coming?" Wendy asked. She assumed that wherever the boys went, Tiger Lily did as well.

Tiger Lily shook her head. "No," she answered. "That's their home. Not mine. And not yours, either, I don't think."

The girl's words surprised Wendy. Somehow, Tiger Lily sensed what she had been thinking, even if she had dared not let herself say it aloud—until then. "I don't know where my home is, exactly. Or where I want it to be."

"You will," Tiger Lily said.

Dismounting, Tiger Lily rubbed her hand gently over her horse's powerful neck. Then she walked to Wendy. Her voice was serious but soft as she began to speak. "The first time I rode out on my own, my grandmother came to me and said: *Feel the ground beneath your feet, so that your eyes might find the stars. Hold the past in your heart but know that where you go from here is up to you.*"

Wendy followed Tiger Lily's gaze up into the star-studded sky. The two girls were silent. Wendy heard the rustle of animals in the woods nearby and the soft whisper of the wind through the trees. Tiger Lily's grandmother was right. By looking up, Wendy felt grounded. But she still wasn't sure where her heart was leading—not yet, at least.

"Thank you," Wendy finally said, letting out a deep breath. "For helping me today."

Tiger Lily laughed, the sound strange in the quiet woods. "*They* need my help," she said, gesturing to the door. "But not you. When their whole world feels upside down, you'll be the one to right it."

Leaving her mysterious words to hang in the air, Tiger Lily turned and mounted her horse. The magnificent creature reared back, shaking its head as it whinnied. "Sleep tight, Wendy Moira Angela Darling. We will see each other again."

And with that, she turned and galloped off into the night.

Wendy watched her go, her mind racing. So much had happened in the short time they had been in Neverland. Tiger Lily seemed like a friend, and Wendy didn't like to say goodbye. With a sigh, she looked through the door in the wall. In the distance she heard the echo of laughter and saw a faint flicker of firelight.

While she wasn't sure where she would end up, for now she was going to see what was on the other side of that door. Maybe there would be an answer.

Wendy meandered down a long dark corridor. The meager light that had shone in from the doorway behind her soon faded altogether. Her breath quickened, and she moved faster and faster down the hall, following the faint flickering light from above.

Wendy had never been a huge fan of the dark. Too many stories, perhaps. An overactive imagination, maybe. But to her, the dark had always represented the monsters that lay under the bed or hid in the closet. It was beginning to seem a bit too spooky, and just when she was sure she would scream, the corridor ended.

As Wendy stepped out, her fears quickly gave way to wonder. She found herself in the most amazing space she had ever seen: the inside of the Lost Boys' lair. The corridor had taken her into the castle she had seen from outside the wall. And it was just as amazing on the inside.

The only word Wendy could find to describe the place was *grand*. Trees grew up out of the wide floorboards and wound their way in and out of huge windows that framed the main hall of the castle. Moss covered the stone, and vines hung, creating natural rope swings. In the center, a spiral staircase twisted up toward the tower high above, like something out of a fairy tale, a castle time had forgotten—but the Lost Boys had made their home. And with the vines and trees and crumbling stone to crawl

over, it made for an oversize playground of sorts. It was perfect for a bunch of children with no rules to follow besides their own.

Hearing a joyous shout, Wendy looked up just in time to see Tootles slide down a makeshift zip line. Dropping to the ground right in front of her, he smiled.

"How did you find this place?" Wendy asked.

"Peter found it," Tootles replied. "He brought me here, just like he did all of us. . . ."

Wendy nodded. "Just like he brought me."

"Exactly," Tootles said, his grin widening. Then, gesturing for her to follow, Tootles led Wendy out of the main room and down a long hall to another huge room. A fire roared in the fireplace, warming the space and casting long shadows on the walls. Old portraits, long since faded, hung on the walls, and in the center of it all sat Peter, presiding over the group. He lounged on an oversize chair, with its fabric ripped and torn but nevertheless impressive. Scanning the room, Wendy saw her brothers. Michael was with the mysterious and masked Bellweather, who was patching Mr. Bear back together, using a spoon for the missing arm. He held it out to Michael, and the younger boy quickly pulled the stuffed animal to his chest.

"Mr. Bear says thank you very much!"

A hint of a smile flashed under Bellweather's partial face mask as John quickly thrust his pocket watch at him.

"Do you think you could fix this, too?" John asked.

Bellweather took the pocket watch from John and turned it over in his hand. The watch was shattered, its hands no longer moving. He examined it, his eyes serious and his touch on the metal gentle. Then he looked up at John and nodded. John smiled, relief flooding his face. Wendy knew how upset her brother must be about the watch. It was, after all, their father's, and he would not take kindly to having it returned in anything but pristine condition. She was glad Bellweather could help.

Pulling her gaze from her brothers, Wendy saw that the watch was not the only thing in need of repair. The room sorely needed cleaning. But then she realized that there wasn't just a random mess in the space. Remnants of the Lost Boys' childhoods littered the floors and surfaces. A tin soldier lay on the ground near a rag doll. An old magazine with a pirate ship on the cover was flung on a table. As Wendy reached to pick it up, Curly stopped her.

"Wendy, Wendy—can you tell us a bedtime story now?" she asked.

"Yes!" the twins cried. "Bedtime stories!"

"We've been waiting forever," added Nibs.

Wendy smiled and took a seat close to the fire. The children rushed toward her, pushing and shoving to get closer. Some sat, others kneeled, but all looked eager for their story.

"I could. But actually . . ." Wendy said when everyone was settled. "I was thinking . . . perhaps *Peter* could tell us a story first."

Peter looked up, startled. He looked back and forth between Tinker Bell and Wendy and then shrugged, as if that was an obvious request and one he didn't mind.

"What about?" he finally asked.

Wendy chose her words carefully. Ever since Curly had hinted that Hook hadn't always been the way he was now, she had been waiting for a chance to get some answers. This seemed like the perfect opportunity.

"Oh," she said, trying to sound casual. "About how you came to Neverland, maybe. And how you met . . . Captain Hook?"

Peter frowned. "It's a very short story," he said. "It goes like this: I fought Captain Hook in a duel, and I cut off his—"

Wendy stopped him. "Yes, yes, everyone knows that part. But how did you meet him? Why did you start fighting in the first place?"

The Lost Boys' heads whipped back and forth between Peter and Wendy. They were unsure of what was going on. No one ever questioned Peter. But Wendy was doing just that. There was tension in the room none of them had ever felt before.

"Because," Peter snapped, "he's a pirate and I'm Peter Pan."

Wendy shook her head. "It can't be as simple as that," she said, pressing him.

"Why not?" asked Peter.

"Because nothing ever is." Once she started, Wendy couldn't stop. All the things she had been wondering about rushed out.

"Where did you both come from? Where are his mother and father? Where are yours?"

Finally, Peter shouted, "Ah, but that's a trick question! This is Neverland, where there *are* no mothers and fathers."

The room quieted as Peter's words echoed off the walls and hit the Lost Boys. He had meant them to be playful, but his tone had a cold edge to it that made everyone shift uncomfortably.

"But why aren't there?" Birdie said softly, finally breaking the silence.

"I don't remember my mother," Slightly added.

"Well, now you don't have to. Wendy can be our mother!" Curly suggested.

"Oh, yes! Can you, Wendy?" asked Nibs.

Wendy felt a wave of guilt. She hadn't meant to make the Lost Boys sad; she just wanted to know more about Peter.

"Oh, goodness, no!" she said, trying to be gentle. "I don't even know if I want to be a mother."

The Lost Boys' faces dropped, and Wendy rushed on, trying to right the ship. "But I still have one, and so do all of you, somewhere out there. I'm sure they love you . . . and . . . and miss you."

Her voice faded, and she felt Peter's angry gaze on her. Had she gone too far?

"I wouldn't mind seeing my mother again . . ." Tootles said.

Peter leapt up, his clenched fists on his hips. "Yes you would!"

he shouted. "Because seeing your mother again would mean going back to the real world, which would mean growing up!"

He snapped his mouth shut, realizing what he had just said—the door he had just opened. The Lost Boys looked at each other. They had never considered the possibility before.

"*Could* we go back?" Nibs asked Wendy. "If we wanted to?"

"Yeah, could we?" Birdie repeated. It was impossible not to hear the hope in her voice.

"Sure," Peter snarled before Wendy could respond. "If you want to wind up like Hook."

As he spoke, he stared daggers at Wendy. She had ruined what should have been a celebration. He had defeated the pirates and saved the day—again. And instead of hearing a story and having a lovely evening, they were talking about growing up. He hated it.

With a huff, he flew out of the room, disappearing from sight. A moment later there was a loud thud as, somewhere above them, Peter slammed his door.

An uncomfortable silence fell over the room. Even Wendy fidgeted. She knew that she was part of the problem. Wendy and Peter were the oldest there. They were supposed to be role models. But Peter was acting like a spoiled child. Even Tinker Bell seemed to think so, because though her gaze had followed Peter as he fled the room, she did not go chasing after him.

The Lost Boys looked—and probably felt—the same way Wendy did whenever she overheard her parents fighting.

"Oh, dear," she finally said, sighing.

Slightly frowned. "Never good when Peter starts slamming doors."

"I'm sorry I asked for a story," Curly added, kicking at the ground.

Wendy looked at the sad faces of the Lost Boys. "No, no," she said. "It's not your fault. How about . . ." She paused, trying to think of something she could do to make up for the scene that had just unfolded. Suddenly, she had an idea. "How about I sing you a song instead? This is something my mother sings me and my brothers sometimes. . . ."

And with that, Wendy began to sing, softly at first, but her voice strengthened as she saw the wonder and then the happiness that washed over the faces of the children.

Beautiful, and a tad bittersweet, as lullabies sometimes were, the song carried through the room and up the stairs. In his room, Peter heard the song and felt a stirring in his heart he hadn't felt for ages. Angrily, he brushed it off.

Unaware, Wendy kept singing, happy to bring some childhood joy to the Lost Boys. And as her happiness grew, the song swelled still louder, floating out the broken windows of the castle and up over the trees into the dark of night. . . .

CHAPTER ELEVEN

Leading his crew through the very same woods, Captain Hook was busy thinking—about all the ways he was finally going to put an end to Peter and his irksome band. But his thoughts were suddenly interrupted by the faintest sound of song.

"Do you hear that?" Hook asked. He stopped walking and strained his ears, listening hard. All around him, his crew did the same, picking the melody out of the air. Some began to smile as the song tickled their hearts. A few even tried to hum the tune. Of them all, though, Hook seemed the most lost in the song.

His expression softened. "What is that?"

"Fruit bats," said Smee, who didn't have his ear horn with him and could not hear what everyone else heard. "They're common this time of year. . . ."

Hook shook his head impatiently. "No! Not that," he snapped. "Listen. Do you hear it?"

Smee grabbed a rag, stuffed it in his ear, and gave it a quick turn. His ear clean—or rather, cleaner than it had been—Smee

held up his head again. The faint tune drifted over him, causing him to smile like the others.

"Oh, that! Yes," he said. "I don't know what that is."

"I've heard something like it once before, methinks," Hook said, almost wistful. His eyes had a dreamy, faraway look— almost like something was fluttering around happily in his stomach. It was most unsettling.

"Whereabouts?" Smee asked, noticing that his captain seemed off.

"It's been so long I don't recall," Hook admitted. "I would that I could, but I cannot. I think, maybe, it was something good . . . something right. . . ."

"Perhaps it was a dream," Smee suggested.

"It must have been. And yet . . ." Hook's voice drifted off as the melody continued to echo through the woods. For a long moment, all the pirates just stood there, lost in the strange feelings overwhelming them. The song tugged at a part of each that he had long since thought gone. What that was, none of them could voice. But none wanted the moment to end.

As the last notes of the song faded, Hook shook his head, as if coming out of a dream. He realized what the song meant to him.

"*This* is what the boy's been keeping from me," he said, his voice tight.

"Singing?" Smee asked.

"No," Hook said. And then, his voice cracking with emotion, he uttered a single word: "Joy."

Inside the castle, Wendy stopped singing. One by one, the children had all drifted off to sleep, lulled into dreamland by Wendy's soft song. Their eyes had closed, their breathing had evened, and soon the room was silent but for an occasional soft snore or mumbled word.

Looking up, Wendy saw that the only one still awake was Tinker Bell. The little fairy went to her and chimed gently. Wendy strained, as usual, to make sense of what Tinker Bell was saying.

"I wish I could understand you, Tinker Bell," she said sadly. The fairy nodded in response. There was so much she thought the fairy might tell her, so many things Tinker Bell might have to say—about Neverland, about Peter. "I don't think Peter understands you, either, does he? Or at least he doesn't listen."

Tinker Bell shook her head. It seemed to pain her to admit that the boy they both admired didn't listen as well as he could. But they both knew it to be true. Peter was Peter. He listened to himself—and that was it.

"Well, that's his loss," Wendy said, "not yours. I bet you have the most wonderful things to say."

The little fairy nodded happily, and for the first time

since they had met, Wendy felt they were coming to an understanding—perhaps even a friendship, of sorts. Tinker Bell seemed to think something over and then gestured for Wendy to follow. The fairy led her to the stairs and, sprinkling pixie dust as she went, lit the way forward.

At the very top, they came to a large wooden door. Carved into the planks were the words *PETER'S ROOM*. Wendy smiled. The words were written in a boy's hand, the letters large and wobbly. Peering closer, Wendy noticed something else written below Peter's name. It was another name. Or at least it used to be a name. It was now covered in deep scratches, making it almost unreadable. But Wendy could just make it out.

"James?" she read aloud. Then she looked at Tinker Bell. "Who is . . . ?"

With a flick of her wrist, Tinker Bell painted a shape in the air with gold dust. Wendy gasped as the image grew clear: a hook.

"Oh . . ." she said as everything clicked into place. Curly had mentioned that Hook hadn't always been as he had become. But now Wendy realized that not only was that true, but he and Peter had been friends—at least once upon a time.

Taking a deep breath, Wendy pushed open the door and walked into a huge attic. Part of the roof had caved in, revealing a breathtaking view of Neverland beyond. The other half of the room was decorated in an assortment of furniture that was all

worn and broken. But despite their condition, the items were unmistakable. This room had once been a nursery.

On the far side of the room, close to the where the roof had collapsed, Peter sat with his back to the door. Wendy looked at Tinker Bell. She was unsure what to do next. Should she talk to him? Or go? Waving her hands, Tinker Bell signaled for her to do the former. So Wendy slowly approached the boy. He was playing with something in his hands but paused when she came into view.

"What's that you've got there?" she asked softly.

Peter held up an acorn. He had threaded an old piece of string through it to make it a pendant.

"It's a kiss," he said sadly. "I was going to give it to you so we'd both have one."

"Thank you," Wendy said, taking it. She put it around her neck and smiled. It was sweet of him, even if most of his other actions thus far had been misguided.

"I really thought you'd be happy here," he said, finally meeting her gaze.

"I did, too," Wendy admitted. Neverland was supposed to be the answer to her problems—a way to avoid home and the future. But now that she was there . . . "It's not exactly what I was expecting. It's much more . . . real."

Peter looked surprised. "Of course it's real," he said. "It's just a different real. A better real."

Wendy knew that he believed what he was saying. But could fighting all the time truly be better than her "real" life? Especially when the person you were fighting hadn't always been a sworn enemy? Thinking about the names etched on the door, she couldn't help asking, "Captain Hook was a friend of yours, wasn't he?"

Peter's head jerked up. "Who told you that?"

Wendy flushed. "No one! I just . . ."

"He was my *best* friend," he said, correcting her earlier question. "We ran away from home together, and once we found our way here, we swore we'd never go back, no matter what. We made a promise . . . and he broke it."

Peter's face was awash with emotions as he spoke. Wendy's question had opened a floodgate, and things he had long since stopped thinking about had come rushing back. The boy had been hiding from his past and from his emotions for so long, and now he had to confront the biggest betrayal of his life all over again.

Wendy could tell the pain was intense. Still, she wanted to know more.

"How?" she asked.

"He left," Peter said. "He sailed away one morning without a word. He left me all alone. And when he finally returned, the friend I knew was gone. He'd turned cruel. Evil."

Peter's tone reminded her of her brothers' when they were telling a story to their parents. There was a touch of exaggeration to everything that made it slightly hard to believe, though there were nuggets of truth.

"Was he, though?" she asked. "Or had he just grown up?"

Peter looked aghast. "What's the difference?"

She knew it was best not to push that any further. Looking out over Neverland, she waited a moment and then softly asked, "Don't you think—Do you ever wonder if there might be more to you than what you are right now?"

As she spoke, she thought of her own mother and father, urging her to move on, and she felt a twinge of guilt. She had been so quick to anger when they had said such things. But now . . .

"No," Peter said. "This is me, and that's all there is."

"Why don't you come be you in London, then?" Wendy suggested. "With us?"

Peter didn't hesitate. "If I did that, I'd just be another boy."

"For a while," Wendy admitted.

"And then I'd die."

Wendy couldn't help laughing at the overdramatic answer. He really was much like her brothers: prone to exaggeration and stubborn to a fault.

"Well, I bet there'd be a whole lot more that would happen in between," she said. "Think about . . . all the things that could be right around the corner that you're missing out on." She waited a beat and then added, "And think about what the world is missing out on with you not doing them."

She let her words sink in, both for Peter's sake and her own. She realized that in a way, she was giving herself the same speech. Growing up was inevitable. But it didn't have to be horrible.

Standing up, Wendy looked at Peter one last time. He refused to meet her eye, and she knew she had pushed enough for one evening. She could stay, try to talk to him more. But she thought of her own mother, trying to get her to see how leaving her own nursery was the right thing to do. Sometimes it didn't matter how much love was behind the message. You just weren't willing to hear it. Peter needed time to think. And she would give it to him, just as her mother had done for her.

"Good night, Peter," she said, and then turned and left his room.

She was lost in thought as she made her way down the long staircase, and at first she didn't notice that the lair seemed darker, quieter. The children's even breathing was gone, replaced by silence, and the candles had all been snuffed out. As she reached the bottom of the stairs, her eyes finally adjusted to the dark. And when they did, she gasped.

The children were all bound and gagged, captured by pirates. And then, out of the darkness, a familiar voice rang out.

"Wendy. Moira. Angela. Darling. The little sing-along girl

from London, England. Your voice called me back to my old home."

Hook emerged from the shadows and sneered down at her, twisting his face.

Wendy opened her mouth to scream. But before she could, a large hand clamped down over her face, muffling the noise.

They were caught. And Peter was alone—and unprepared for the battle to come.

CHAPTER TWELVE

In the attic, Peter stared down at the thimble kiss in his hand. His conversation with Wendy played over and over in his head. For the first time in a while, he was questioning everything: Neverland, Hook, himself. He didn't like the feeling one bit. Hearing a familiar chime, he looked over and saw Tinker Bell. She had been watching him silently ever since Wendy left, but now she jingled again. Peter frowned. Her message was clear. Wendy was right, Tinker Bell was telling him. And maybe she was. But he didn't have to like it.

Standing up, he took one last look at the thimble, his first kiss, and then closed his fist around it. Wendy could say what she liked, but he was going to stay here. This was his home. And he wasn't ready to leave it—or grow up. He strode to the door and was about to open it when he happened to glance down. A shadow was on the other side.

Instantly, Peter flew to the rafters and hid in the shadows. Tinker Bell did the same.

The door flew open, and Captain Hook burst inside. "Got you!"

But no one was there. Hook scanned the furniture, which looked vaguely familiar. Not seeing Peter, he lowered his sword.

"Peter?" he called into the room. "Where are you?"

In his hiding spot, Peter narrowed his eyes. Hook had never called him by *just* his first name before. It sounded strange to hear it now, in the room they had once shared as children.

Hook walked about, his hands absently running over the old toys and aged furniture. "How many times did we play hide-and-seek amongst these ruins?" he said, his voice almost wistful. "You were always the best at hiding."

Up in the rafters, Peter and Tinker Bell held their breath. Neither dared move, but Tinker Bell shifted ever so slightly. A minuscule amount of pixie dust floated down in front of Hook. Tinker Bell pressed her hands over her mouth. Had she given them away? Just in case, Peter reached for his sword—only to remember he had left it down on the floor, leaning against a wall. He was defenseless.

Below, Hook narrowed his eyes, and the softer expression faded. His face turned cruel again as he stepped right under them.

"But then again," he said, lifting his own sword once more, "I was always the best at finding you!"

With a shout, he swung his sword up through the air just as Peter jumped down from the rafter.

For one long moment, Peter seemed suspended in the air in front of Hook's sword. And then, in a blur, Hook's sword flew down, leaving a cruel slash across Peter's chest.

Peter gasped and touched his chest. Shock turned to pain as a red shadow blossomed across his green tunic.

Hook was equally surprised. He had never expected to actually hurt Peter. That wasn't how their fights typically went. They were supposed to just fight, back and forth, like they always did. But something was different. Was it that they were in the old nursery? Or perhaps that both had recently given their past more thought? Whatever the reason, things had grown far more serious.

Peter staggered backward, bringing him dangerously close to the caved-in portion of room that led outside. As Peter pulled his hand back from his wound, his face paled. His hand was covered in blood.

"Captain Hook?" he said, lifting his gaze to his enemy.

"Yes, Peter?" Hook replied, his own eyes glued to the wound he had inflicted.

"I don't think I like this adventure . . ." Peter began.

And then his legs gave out and he fell backward off the edge of the parapet, and into the darkness below.

Peter's body seemed to fall in slow motion. He fell down through the branches of the tree that grew out of the floor of the main room of the castle. He thought he saw Wendy's frightened face and heard the usually silent Bellweather's scream as they struggled against the arms of the pirates who held them.

Tinker Bell, a pulsing golden glow, shot through the air with her eyes locked on Peter's falling body. But before she could

reach him, she was snatched from the sky. Smee had trapped her in his hat. As she kicked and raged, the hat seemed to burn in his hand. It turned yellow and gold and red. And then Tinker Bell let out a scream that sounded like a million windows shattering as her heart broke.

A moment later, Peter, with no one left to save him, crashed onto the floorboards. Weak and rotted, they broke apart like toothpicks, and Peter plummeted still farther, then landed with a thud on the cold, hard earth below. There he lay, motionless.

From high above, Hook looked down at the boy, myriad emotions crossing his weathered face. The signs of his long, hard life became more pronounced. His skin seemed to sag, the creases on his face deepened, and a raw, bitter look filled his eyes.

"I've done it," he said. "I killed Peter Pan!"

He was an old man who had fought his last fight.

But what, he wondered, would happen now?

Hook sat in a dinghy, staring absently across the rough waters to another dinghy, which carried the Darling children and the Lost Boys toward the *Jolly Roger*. Since he had left the lair, his thoughts had been scattered, uneven. He saw Wendy rocking herself back and forth and several of the Lost Boys openly weeping. Without their fearless leader, they were lost.

"These things are supposed to be all shiny, aren't they, Cap'n?" Smee asked, interrupting Hook's thoughts. Hook turned and saw that Smee was looking at Tinker Bell, secured in a lantern for safekeeping. "And the shine makes 'em fly?"

Hook lifted the lantern and peered closely at Tinker Bell. She looked worse than the others. Peter's loss had taken a physical toll on her. Her glow was gone, and she seemed to have shrunk in on herself. Her wings hung limp, and there was not a drop of color in her cheeks. Worse still, there was no pixie dust floating around her, no sense at all of any magic.

"Yes," Hook answered. "She used to be far brighter, I think. Or maybe that's just how I remember her."

He sighed heavily.

"C'mon, little fairy," Smee said, giving the lantern a shake. "Make the Cap'n smile."

But Hook pushed the lantern away. "It's not her that troubles me."

Smee looked up, surprised. "Oh—you're talking about the boy, then. But you've bested him. He's gone!"

That was what the captain had always wanted, wasn't it?

Hook nodded. "And now that he is, there's a hole in my heart-stuff. Is it wrong that I feel no joy in his passage? No satisfaction?"

"Killing is a nasty business," Smee answered.

Sighing, Hook looked down at the fairy. Briefly, he felt like her—colorless, without purpose.

"It's so terribly . . . final," he said, more to himself than to Smee. "That's what they don't tell you. All these years, I thought I would feel . . . happy. But now that the deed is done . . . is it possible that I miss him?"

Smee didn't have a good answer for that. So Hook let his gaze drift back to Neverland. He would just have to find something else to fill his time. And as his eyes wandered over the sea toward land, they once again fell on the dinghy with the children inside. Perhaps they would be the answer. . . .

Hook knew that below the decks of the *Jolly Roger*, the children sat huddled together in the dank brig. Sitting in his own quarters, he imagined them there, their thoughts as black as their surroundings. How could they be anything but hopeless? Their leader was gone. They were prisoners of his greatest enemy. And they had no idea what was to become of them.

And to be honest, neither did Hook.

In the early hours of the morning, he was still unsure of what to do next. He flipped absently through papers on his desk, looking for something. In her lantern, Tink sat forlornly, her expression as sad as he imagined the children's to be.

By a cabinet, Smee was mumbling to himself as he pushed several bottles around. He found what he was looking for, and spun around with a large ancient bottle in hand. The writing was

faded, but it appeared to be in French, and the oversize cork was dirty with age. Still, Smee looked pleased.

"It's the time of morning when I'd normally put the kettle on, but . . ." He glanced at the grim look on his captain's face and sighed. "I've been saving this very fine libation all these years, to celebrate your victory, whenever it finally occurred. And now that it's behind us . . ."

He popped the cork, and liquid arched out the top of the bottle. Then he waited hopefully. The captain just needed to find the bright side to all this. And then things could go back to the way they had been. Maybe . . .

Suddenly, Hook sat up straighter. He looked at the spot where Smee stood. He didn't even seem to notice his first mate's attempt to make him happy.

"My list," he said vaguely. "Where is my list?"

"What list?" Smee asked.

"My first list!" Hook said as though it were obvious. "That one I wrote all those years ago. Of all the things I wished to do upon my return to Neverland . . ."

"Ah!" Smee said. "*That* list."

Hook stood up and began to rummage around his quarters, pulling out drawers and sliding open doors. Then he stooped down and looked under his bed. He cried out triumphantly as he retrieved a dusty old scroll. Unrolling it, he saw there was

only one line written on the paper. It read *Kill Peter Pan*. He had remembered there being more than that.

Smee approached the captain and peered at the paper.

"Well, those three words do carry the weight of a lengthier manifesto," he said. "But it's all in the past now."

Hook sighed. It didn't *feel* like it was in the past. It felt quite present. He examined the fairy in her makeshift prison.

"What do you think, Tink?" he asked. "*You* were there at the beginning. Did it have to end like this?"

Tink shook her head.

"I don't know whether or not to believe you," he said. She had always been Peter's friend and biggest fan, never his. Still . . . maybe she was right?

"Captain?" Smee said tentatively. "Remember what you told me back in the woods? When you heard the girl's singsonging? How it made you feel?"

Hook's eyes narrowed. "What did I say?"

"One word . . . one word that could do you good right now . . ."

Intrigued, Hook leaned in and waited for Smee to go on. What was the old man up to? And was he right? Could something do him good after all this?

CHAPTER THIRTEEN

"What's going to happen to us?"

Michael sat huddled beside the other children in the dank, dark brig of the *Jolly Roger*. Through the cracks in the deck shone pale light, by which they could see. But the mood was as dark as the cabin itself.

"Just pray you don't get keelhauled," Curly offered up unhelpfully.

"What's 'keelhauled'?" John asked, stuffing his shaking hands deeper into his pockets.

"You don't want to know," Curly answered.

Birdie, who appeared more fragile and frightened than usual, looked at Curly and frowned. "How do you know what 'keelhauled' means?"

Curly shrugged. "I read about it in a book."

Wendy sat, listening to the others. She knew they were all scared. And why wouldn't they be? They had no idea what was going to happen to them or how they might escape their predicament—or if they ever would at all.

Suddenly, the hatch to the brig swung open and Hook appeared. He thudded down the stairs followed closely by Smee, who held Tinker Bell in the lantern. The children shuffled back against the far wall, and a few let out frightened murmurs.

Walking to the children, Hook waved his hand in the air.

"At ease," he said, locking his eyes on Wendy. "I only want a word with you."

Wendy wanted nothing to do with Hook. Peter might have been hotheaded and stubborn, a bit careless even, but the children loved him. And Hook had taken him from them. She would rather rot in the brig than ever talk to him.

"I have nothing to say to you," she said.

"Then listen," Hook responded. He hummed a tune. It was hard to make out at first, but slowly it became familiar. It was the tune Wendy had been singing to the Lost Boys in the lair before everything went south.

"What is that?" he asked when he finished.

"That?" Wendy said. "It was just . . . That's just a lullaby. . . ."

Hook brushed off her vague explanation. "It reminds me of something. Where does it come from?"

"I—"

"Tell me! Why does it make me feel so?"

Wendy was surprised to see anguish and uncertainty in Hook's eyes. The man had always seemed so angry, so dangerous. But now he looked like a child whose teddy had been taken from him.

To her surprise, she felt a pang of sympathy. "I couldn't say. It's just—it's something my mother sings us. . . ."

"Your who?" Captain Hook said.

"My mother," Wendy repeated, surprised that the word seemed foreign to Hook. Had he really been gone for so long that he had forgotten what a mother was? No wonder he was so cold and heartless, without a mother's love and support to guide him, without her songs to soothe him.

Suddenly, Hook seemed lost in memory. "Of course."

Realizing that she had a sliver of an opening to appeal to whatever decency the man had left, she took a chance.

"I know you weren't always like this, Captain Hook," she said softly. "I know you and Peter were friends. I've heard the stories."

Hook leaned in. "Have you?" he said. "And what happens in those stories?"

Wendy swallowed nervously. She looked to the Lost Boys for encouragement. They nodded for her to go on. "You . . . you left Neverland. And when you returned, you were . . ."

"Evil?" Hook finished for her.

Wendy nodded. "Yes."

"Hmmm," Hook murmured, not as upset by the description as Wendy would have expected. "There is truth to that. But he left out the most important part. I didn't just *leave* Neverland . . ."

Wendy didn't need him to finish. She knew what he was going

to say. She had been piecing it together since she was in Peter's room. Hook hadn't just left Neverland....

"Peter made you go," Wendy said.

A wave of pain, mixed with anger and regret, washed over the pirate's face. "There it is," he said. "That's the sticking point. My once and best friend *banished* me, all because I missed my...my..."

"Your mother?" asked Wendy.

"Yes! Yes, my mother—who once upon a time must have sung me that very song. Is it so terrible a thing to miss a mother?"

Wendy thought of her own mother and the nights in the nursery when she had sung Wendy to sleep, the countless times she had kissed boo-boos and dried tears.

"No. Of course it's not," she said.

In an instant, Hook's face turned icy again, and he once more resembled the fearsome pirate captain he was. "Tell that to your dearly departed friend, then, for he surely thought otherwise."

He began to pace back and forth in front of Wendy, his words coming faster and faster as emotions he had long since buried rose to the surface.

"And do you know that after all that, I never did find her, never made it home, never saw my poor sweet mama again. I left Neverland and was lost at sea. I would have surely perished had I not been saved by this man here." He paused and nodded toward Smee. "So there I was, rescued and raised by pirates, taught to pillage and to kill. By and by, they made me their captain. And I,

in turn, brought them right back here," he finished with a snarl. Reliving those times had pushed aside his softer emotions.

"But why come back at all if Peter hurt you so?" Wendy asked.

"Because . . . he was my friend," Hook said after a moment. "And I was happy here."

"You could be happy again," Wendy said.

Hook shook his head. "No. My time for joy is lost. Hurt and fear are all I have now. All the things I wanted to do have passed me by. Everything I could have been has been reduced to this. This, Wendy Moira Angela Darling, is what growing up looks like."

Wendy stared at the man and realized that he genuinely believed what he was saying. But she also realized, with surprise, that she was wiser than this bitter, sad pirate.

"No, it doesn't," she said. "This is what happens when you grow up wrong."

Fury came over Hook's face, and he whipped his hook through the air. He had had enough. "Find me a child who truly knows the difference between right and wrong, and I'll show you a man who's forgotten why it ever mattered in the first place."

Turning and stomping to Smee and the others waiting by the stairs, he shouted out, "Execute every last one of them!"

"But, Captain," Smee started. He stopped and then started again. "James—don't you think—"

Hook whipped around, fury in his face as he gazed down at his first mate. "Never call me that. I am Captain Hook!"

A moment later, pirates flooded into the cabin to take the children. Wendy watched in horror as Mrs. Starkey, a large old ogre of a pirate, grabbed Michael's arm.

"This one first," the pirate sneered. "He smells the worst."

Tears pricked at Wendy's eyes as the woman began to drag her youngest brother away. Near him, John tried, and failed, to help. Wendy couldn't let this happen. Peter wasn't there to save them, but she had to at least try.

"Wait!" she yelled. Her voice pierced the air, and everyone stopped. "Take me! But let them live. They're only children, after all. They'll grow up to be good pirates, every last one of them. Especially that one."

She pointed at John and gave him a look, begging him with her eyes to stay quiet.

In the lantern, Tinker Bell, surprised by Wendy's selfless act, lifted her head from her arms. She felt a stirring of hope . . . and her defeat began to turn into anger.

Meanwhile, Hook stared at Wendy, considering her offer. Then he shrugged.

"Your largesse is admirable," he said. "Perhaps it will lead to a bigger splash."

He nodded at Mrs. Starkey, and the woman dropped her hold on Michael and headed toward Wendy.

"Wendy, no!" John shouted. "You can't. . . ."

"Yes, I can," Wendy said, trying to sound convincing even

though she was shaking like a leaf. "I'm your big sister. Be brave, boys. And if you see Mother again, tell her I—"

And then, as the brig filled with the shouts and cries of the Lost Boys, Wendy was hauled up onto the deck to meet her fate.

Dawn's early light was just filtering into the lagoon. There were shadows on the mist and fog that rose off the warm water surrounding the *Jolly Roger*. On board the ship, several pirates banged on the bottoms of barrels, adding a steady drumbeat to the events unfolding.

Wendy stared at the large plank that had been laid out over the edge of the *Jolly Roger*'s deck. She felt the eyes of the pirates and the Lost Boys on her back. The pirates were cheering for her demise, while the Lost Boys were mostly quiet, a few sniffling every now and then. Wrapped in heavy chains, she had no hope that once she hit the water she would do anything but sink.

Feeling the not-so-gentle touch of a harpoon on her back, Wendy took a deep breath and stepped onto the plank. As she walked its length, the wood bent slightly under her weight. The clapping and cheering got louder behind her as Wendy reached the end of the plank. She looked down at the deep, dark water, her toes curling around the edge of the wood.

"Farewell, Wendy Moira Angela Darling," Hook said, his words anything but kind.

Wendy teetered on the edge of the board, her mind whirling. She wanted to turn back and take one last look at her brothers, but she didn't dare.

Her only chance now, and it was a sliver of one, was that any remnants of pixie dust might help her fly.

"Think happy thoughts," she murmured under her breath.

Then, inhaling deeply, Wendy jumped.

At the very same time, unbeknownst to the pirates, Tinker Bell burst free of her lantern. She had watched every moment and seen Wendy's heart. It had given the little fairy the strength to find her glow again after losing Peter. She had no intention of losing Wendy, too.

But Wendy had no idea this was happening. She was falling, fast at first, and then almost in slow motion. She plummeted toward the sea. And as she fell, something strange happened. Instead of seeing her old life flash before her eyes, she saw her future in snippets. She saw herself growing up—reading books with friends; running on the beach; flying in a plane as a young woman; writing stories on a typewriter and napping in the midday sun as an old woman, surrounded by her children and grandchildren. Her life to come, she realized, would have been amazing. Growing up didn't mean losing her sense of adventure. It just meant all-new adventures.

But . . . she would never get to live that future. Because she was still falling and the water was approaching fast.

CHAPTER FOURTEEN

Hook had watched eagerly as Wendy jumped from the plank. He listened, waiting for the telltale splash as her body hit the water.

But no splash came—not even a wave against the boat. Just the sea breeze and seagulls.

Something was very wrong.

Hook cocked his head. "Mr. Smee?"

"Yes?"

"Did you hear a splash?" he asked.

Smee nodded. "Absolutely, Captain," he said, but then his nodding slowed. "It was, well, actually . . ."

"I didn't hear one," another pirate offered up.

"Nor I," said another.

Hook's eyebrows furrowed. "Surely she'd have hit the water by now."

"Yes," Smee agreed. "Unless she fell very slowly."

Hook let out a shout. This was ridiculous. How slowly could a

girl possibly fall? Turning to look at the rest of his crew, he called out, "Did *anyone* hear a splash?"

The pirates shook their heads. No one said no out loud, though, as no one dared ever say that word to the captain.

Hook strode toward the edge of the ship. He leaned over and gasped.

Pixie dust was everywhere, spreading over the boat, rippling across the planks like liquid gold. Hook stepped back, trying to avoid the stuff, but it was impossible. The magic spread like wildfire now, engulfing the deck and rising up the masts. It shimmered over the rigging, and then, with one final pulse, it receded, like a wave, leaving a subtle glow in its wake.

"Why, that looks like . . ." Smee started.

He turned to the lantern he had forgotten all about during Wendy's walk. It was empty. Tinker Bell was gone.

Hook looked at Smee, and then at his crew, and finally at the Lost Boys. They were all smiling. That couldn't be a good thing. What other surprises were in store?

He didn't have to wait long. Suddenly, the glow pulsed and brightened, nearly blinding. Hook squinted in the light. And then he gasped again as Wendy rose into the air. Her chains were gone, replaced by pixie dust. She looked like a golden statue.

Backing up, Hook held his hand in front of his face, as though

that could protect him. "She has the boy's magic!" he said, a little frightened and a little confused.

Tinker Bell chimed, and from the air, Wendy smiled. She knew exactly what the fairy was saying.

"This magic belongs to no boy," she said. She floated over the plank and toward Hook, like a ghost hovering in the air in a haunted house.

Hook slowly backed up some more. "We still have you outnumbered, girl," he said, though his voice was shaky. "Hand over hook over fist. My men will give their lives to save their captain."

Wendy smiled. That was what she had been hoping Hook would say. "But what's a captain without a ship?" she asked as a loud creak echoed over the water and the ship shuddered violently. Everyone threw out their arms, trying to keep their balance as the deck boards quaked and buckled.

And then the *Jolly Roger* began to rise into the air.

With a sucking sound, it lifted out of the sea, sending a torrent of salt water gushing from the hull into the waves below. As the morning sun hit its watery sides, the ship shone, like something out of Wendy's bedtime stories.

Wendy flew to the top of the mast, with Tinker Bell at her side. Together, they unfurled the mainsail. As it lowered, Tinker Bell covered it, too, with pixie dust. When the sails caught the wind, they billowed majestically. The whole ship was now shining and golden.

Craning his head up at the insolent girl and the frustrating fairy, Hook was momentarily stunned silent by the sight of his ship rendered anew. But then he shook his head. Looking at Mr. Smee, he shouted, "Get my ship back into the water!"

"Yes, Captain!" Then Smee frowned. "How, Captain?"

He had never dealt with a flying ship before. A beached one? Yes. A sinking one? Sure. But this was a whole new problem.

"Just do it!" the captain snarled. "Do it as fast as you . . ."

His voice trailed off as he heard a howl in the distance. He whirled toward land. The sound was familiar. He pulled out his spyglass and scanned the horizon.

The Lost Boys had heard the howl, too. Throwing off their ropes, which had been loosened by pixie dust, they raced to the ship's side.

"Is that . . ." Nibs said.

"I think it might be . . ." the twins continued.

"Oh, it definitely is," Tootles said, a huge smile spreading across his face as his gaze landed on the far cliff.

There, galloping along the cliff's edge, was a white stallion. And astride him were none other than Tiger Lily and . . .

"Peter!" Wendy shouted, spotting him from her perch in the crow's nest.

Hearing the shout, Hook whipped his spyglass through the air. When he saw the boy, his eyes widened, and then, to his own surprise, he felt a flood of relief wash over him. Peter Pan

was alive. He was back, ready to fight another day. Hook couldn't wait.

Unable to take his eyes off Peter, he watched as Tiger Lily raced her stallion right toward the cliff's edge. Behind her, Peter stood, his sword lifted high in one hand and Michael's teddy bear clutched in his other. The horse's hooves pounded faster and faster as they got nearer and nearer to the cliff's edge. And then, just before the ground disappeared, Tiger Lily pulled back hard on the reins. Her horse spun on its hindquarters as Peter jumped.

Time seemed to slow down as Peter hovered in the air above the sea and the *Jolly Roger*. With his sword still raised, and the bear still in his hand, he looked the image of a hero racing into battle. And then time sped up again and he fell, faster and faster until he slammed into a sail, driving his sword into the thick fabric. He continued to fall, but slowed down by the fabric, his descent was less frantic. When he reached the bottom of the sail, he dropped effortlessly onto the foredeck.

Taking a deep breath, he straightened up. Then he turned to Hook and, with a smile, said, "Missed me?"

Hook grinned back wickedly. "More than you will ever know," he said. He walked toward Peter. "How did you do it? Faith and trust and pixie dust?"

"No," said Peter. "No pixie dust this time. Just a little help from my friends."

When he was lying there on the cold ground after Hook had

slashed him and he had fallen from the nursery, he had thought he was a goner for sure. But his shadow wouldn't let him go, and it had raced off to find Tiger Lily. Slipping through the dark, the shadow had flown through the woods, finally spotting firelight flickering near the edge of a cliff. Zipping forward, the shadow passed over the wigwams set on the high ground. A few older warriors sat near the chief, Tiger Lily's great-great-grandmother, while children ducked in and out of the firelight. Gazing into the fire, Tiger Lily didn't notice the shadow at first. But as it passed right in front of her, she sensed it and knew that Peter was in trouble. So she had gone to him, as fast as her horse could carry her.

He had never been alone. And that, he realized, was how he had survived: his friends—friends he had not treated in the best manner of late.

Hook took a step closer. Peter did the same. Both were eager to see who would make the first move.

"You dare talk of friends to me," said Hook. "Proud and insolent youth: draw thy sword."

"Sad and sinister man—one last time," Peter said, parrying.

They tapped their swords together, then began to fight. But this was not like any fight they had ever had before. This fight wasn't for fun. It was full of emotion, more a brawl than a dance. This was *the* fight—the one in which every unspoken thought and feeling would be revealed. Hook had lifted his sword high above his head, ready to bring it down, when a shadow crossed

his face. He looked up just in time to see the mainsail falling toward him. A moment later, he, Peter, and everyone below them were covered by the fabric.

Up in the crow's nest, Wendy and Tinker Bell looked down to see if their distraction had worked. But it hadn't. The two enemies cut themselves free and began to battle all over the deck, weaving among the pirates and the Lost Boys, who had taken up their own fight.

"Just like old times, isn't it?" Hook said as they made their way up onto the quarterdeck.

"All your times are old," Peter shot back.

A pirate ran at him with an ax, but an arrow struck him in the hand, and he stopped in his tracks: Curly had come to the rescue. The Lost Boy jumped down from the rigging and gave Peter a smile before racing off to help others.

Once more, Hook and Peter were caught up in their own fight. Michael was struggling to get his bear back from the pirates who had grabbed it, while Slightly and Nibs had spotted the huge cannon and moved toward it with cannonballs in hand. While Wendy tried to help her brothers, Smee was face to face with the twins, who had stolen his tea and then, to his horror, dumped it all over the floor of the ship.

He let out a shout and was on the verge of tears when he heard a familiar chime behind him. Turning, he saw Tinker Bell.

Lifting his hands in the air, he said, "I didn't want to hurt anyone. I just . . . I just . . . I just want to fly."

Tinker Bell looked surprised. And then, to *Smee's* surprise, the fairy shrugged and blew a handful of dust right in his face. He sneezed, the reaction blowing him clean off his feet—and into the air. With a happy shout, he sailed up over the ship. From there he watched as the fighting continued. It really was a bird's-eye view. He spotted Tiger Lily climbing up the anchor onto the ship, which was still floating above the water—though it had turned and now headed toward the rocky cliffs. Tiger Lily quickly joined the fray, clearly a practiced warrior, but Smee could do little from way up where he was. So he shrugged and continued to watch.

Grabbing the helm, John and Michael tugged, desperately trying to turn the ship as it headed toward the cliffs. At the last moment, Tinker Bell flew in, giving the ship another burst of pixie dust. With a creak and a groan, the ship moved, scraping along the cliff. There was an ear-piercing shriek as rock met wood.

After battling her way free of a clutch of pirates, Wendy joined her brothers at the helm. Several pirates fell over the side of the boat—only to be captured by mermaids and dragged under the water. A few others had slipped and been knocked unconscious. Wendy barely gave them a glance. The ship needed to get free of the rocks and out to safety.

Grabbing the wheel tightly, she yelled out, "Everyone, hold on to something! We're going for a little ride."

And then, as the children grabbed anything they could hold on to—ropes, rails, masts—she gave the wheel one huge spin, sending the boat pitching wildly. As she and the others hung on for dear life, Peter and Hook continued their fight.

CHAPTER FIFTEEN

Oblivious to the larger danger they faced, Peter and Hook had moved their fight into the captain's quarters. In the darkness of the cabin, Hook lost sight of Peter and paused. But it didn't take long for him to spot a familiar shadow hovering near one of his maps. He smiled. This was one of Peter's many tricks: sending his shadow in one direction while he went in another. Still, Hook couldn't help himself. He went after the shadow.

At the same moment, he heard soft footsteps behind him, and then he felt something slam down over his head. Reaching up, he realized that Peter had placed a crocodile skull on him. He yanked it off just as the boat tilted violently, sending him and Peter sliding across the floor. Hook heard screams outside as the ship continued to tilt and then changed direction. As the cabin pitched, Peter and Hook attempted to fight. But mostly they just tried to stay upright as the ship slowly kept tilting farther and farther until it was upside down, the mast pointing to the sea below, the bottom of the ship to the sky.

Still, they would not give up their fight completely. It meant too much to both of them.

Leaping up toward a beam on the ceiling, Peter narrowly missed being stabbed by Hook's sword. Then the captain swiped at him with his hook—but instead of hitting Peter, it sank into the beam and became stuck. Angrily, Hook tried to free himself, but the hook was buried tight. He tugged. He pulled. He yanked, until finally with a pop the hook came free. The momentum sent Hook tumbling back toward a skylight that, with the tilt of the ship, was more like a trapdoor. With a crash, he broke through it and plummeted toward the sea—but was stopped by the rear sail. He bounced on the fabric before crawling to and hauling himself onto the mast, grimacing.

Peering down through the broken skylight, Peter saw his enemy far below. He also clearly saw how upside down everything was. If he hadn't been so intent on finishing his fight, he would have found the whole thing jolly good fun. But now was not the time.

Putting his leg through the window, he started to climb out. He had barely gotten free of the shattered glass when his foot slipped. He flapped his arms only to remember that he didn't have the power of pixie dust. It was useless. Gravity overtook him, and he began to fall.

"Gotcha!"

He was jolted to a stop by a hand grabbing his. Looking up,

he smiled. Wendy was holding on to him. She floated in midair with the same ease he had once known. A look passed between the two of them, an unspoken apology, a nod of forgiveness. And then, as she held his hand, a small amount of pixie dust sprinkled onto his fingers. It wasn't much. But it was enough. Giving her a nod, he pulled his hand free and drifted down through the air to the spot where Hook clung to the mast.

Hovering in front of him, Peter watched as the man hauled himself slowly, painfully back up the mast toward the deck above.

"Do you know what hurts the most about growing old?" Hook asked, his breath uneven. "It's not the creaky bones or dashed dreams or the sense of death drawing ever nearer. It's knowing your best friend can look you in the eyes and not recognize you."

The ship turned again, righting itself bit by bit. The mast pointed first to the horizon and then upward once more. The sails righted themselves, and pirates who had managed to stay aboard now fell to the decks, happy to be right side up.

"You're the one who wanted to leave!" Peter shouted. He had known ever since he woke up on the cold ground that this conversation was inevitable. Now that Hook's memory had been jogged, he wouldn't let it go. He would never stop this fight.

"I was a child!" Hook protested.

Peter lifted an eyebrow. "Look what you've become."

"Fate lent me this hand," Hook said, nodding toward his hook.

"Fate *took* your hand," Peter said, correcting him.

Hook shook his head. No. That was wrong. The boy had it all wrong.

"It was all you!" he shouted.

Realizing they were upright, he pulled his hook from the mast and lifted his sword high above his head. He wanted to finish this fight—once and for all.

But to his surprise, Peter raised his own hands in surrender. "Stop!"

Hook stared angrily at Peter. There was no way he was going to back down now. He had to fight. This was what they were supposed to do—now and forever. He had felt the emptiness of his life without Peter in it. He hadn't liked it. So he would continue to fight him, as they were meant to do.

"Don't give up now, boy!" he said. "Imagine a Neverland without the two of us, without our battles and our brawls. Without you, the fire that fuels me would go out"—as he spoke, he brought his sword down over and over right in front of Peter, pushing him back up against the mast—"and without that fire, you would have no choice but to—"

"Be a real boy?" Peter finished.

Hook startled and then shook his head. "No! A real boy would grow. A real boy would . . ."

Once more, Peter finished the sentence. "Apologize?"

Now Hook was flummoxed. He hadn't been expecting that. "For what?"

"For hurting you," Peter said, all joking aside, all bitterness gone. "For being a rotten friend."

Dying, or nearly dying, had woken something in Peter: a feeling long since dormant—empathy. He had felt emptiness and fear, just like he knew Hook must have felt years earlier when he longed to return to his home. For so long, Peter had just wanted to fight Hook because he was mad at him. But now he realized he hadn't been mad. He had been hurt, too. He had felt lonely and scared. And he didn't want to feel that way anymore.

He dropped his sword, and it fell to the deck, landing next to Wendy, who was staring up at the pair. "I'm sorry I did what I did, Captain Hook. I'm sorry I hurt you, James."

Hook was stunned silent. But only for a moment.

"You don't get to do that!" he screamed. "That's not how this works. I need you to fight!"

"But this isn't fun anymore," Peter said.

He looked down at Wendy and the Lost Boys, at Tinker Bell and Tiger Lily—his friends. *They* had fun. *They* had adventures. And they were always better together.

"It's not supposed to be fun!" Hook shouted, all his patience gone.

He was done with this new game Peter seemed to be playing

at. The boy was full of hot air. Hook lifted his sword high above his head and moved to bring it down.

But before he could, Wendy and Tinker Bell landed between them, blocking his blow.

"Oh, Captain," Wendy said, shaking her head, "grow up."

And then, before Hook could sputter a retort, there was a terrible boom.

Down on the deck, the Long Tom, the ship's largest and most powerful cannon, sat smoking. Slightly sat on the ground beside it, a bit dazed from the explosion but nevertheless with a smile on his face. He watched as the cannonball shot through the air and right through the foremast. Like a tree in the forest, the small mast creaked and groaned and then fell, the force slamming it into the mainmast.

As the two masts collided, Hook was thrown off and tumbled through the air toward the sea below. But suddenly someone reached out and stopped his downward trajectory. Looking up, he saw Peter smiling down at him with his hand grasping Hook's hook.

"Gotcha," Peter said.

Hook's eyes were filled with terror as the ship creaked and buckled beneath him. Peter struggled to keep him afloat with the little pixie dust magic he had left. But Hook was a grown man and heavy. It was hard. He could only help if Hook did the one thing that he likely had not done in quite some time.

"Just think happy thoughts!" Peter shouted at him.

Hook closed his eyes hard, straining to think of something, anything, that might resemble a happy time. It seemed to pain him, and Peter felt his own flash of pain. Was finding a good memory truly that hard? Had all their years of fighting erased the memories of make-believe in the woods? Hide-and-seek in the lair? Was this what he had done to Hook?

Opening his eyes, Hook shook his head.

"I haven't got any!" he said at last.

"Yes, you do," Peter insisted, unwilling to let the moment end like this. Hook *had* to have a good memory. Even just one.

But before he could say another word, there was a loud pop, and he felt Hook's weight vanish. Looking down, he saw that he still held Hook's hook, but the captain had slipped out of it.

"No!" Peter shouted, his voice full of anguish, as he watched Hook flail—and then plummet. With a splash, Hook hit the water and then disappeared beneath the frothy waves.

Peter floated down to the deck and stood on shaky legs. His shoulders trembled and tears pricked his eyes as he looked over the railing at the dark swirl of water where Hook had vanished. Pulling his gaze back to the hook in his hand, he shuddered.

"What's wrong, Peter?" a small voice asked, startling him.

Turning, he saw that all the children had gathered near him on the deck. The ship was theirs. The few pirates who had not fallen off the ship during the tumult were cowering in corners or

twisted into balls, shaking with fear. Wendy stood to the side, her eyes filled with her own tears. She had witnessed it all and knew what was wrong.

"He was my friend," Peter said softly. He realized now that the man always had been, in a weird way. And now Peter would never see him again.

The children were silent as they watched Peter mourn. But then, ever so slowly, they moved closer, tightening the circle around him.

"We're your friends, too, Peter," Curly said gently.

Slightly nodded. "We're here for you," he added.

Peter looked at the children. They were right. He had spent so much time focused on Hook that he had never realized just how many good friends he had right in front of him. And now he needed to do what a true friend would do and make the ultimate sacrifice.

"Don't you think it's high time we got you all home?" he asked.

The children looked at each other, unsure if Peter was serious. But he had Tinker Bell cover the ship in pixie dust once more, and as they lifted higher into the air above Neverland, they realized he was completely serious.

"Where to, Peter?" Slightly asked as they gathered near the helm. The sky had brightened, and the stars were fading fast.

Peter looked up and pointed. He might not know how to be

the best friend, but at least he knew this: "Second star to the right and straight on till—"

John cut him off. "Wait, wouldn't it be left?" he asked.

"What?" Peter asked, cocking his head.

"The star," John said. "If we're going back in the opposite direction..."

As Peter and the children began to debate what the right direction was, Wendy watched with a sad smile on her face. She was glad to be going home, but she was going to miss this. Glancing back at Neverland, she squinted. A white horse raced along the beach, and sitting atop the creature was Tiger Lily. The horse reared back, and the girl waved at her. Wendy held a hand up and waved back.

Yes, she thought, she was going to miss this and the friends she had made. Tiger Lily had taught her to be strong. Peter had taught her to be compassionate. And Tinker Bell had shown her how to listen. They were all a part of her life now. But it was time to go home. And while she knew she might never return, at least she would always have the stories.

Feeling a small hand in hers, she looked down and saw Michael. He was clutching his bear in his other hand.

"Say goodbye to Neverland, Mr. Bear," he said softly. "You'll be back home soon."

Wendy gave his hand a squeeze. Yes, they would be back home very soon. And she couldn't wait.

CHAPTER SIXTEEN

Wendy slowly shut the nursery door behind her and turned toward the stairs. The Darling house was quiet and peaceful, and she stood for a moment, enjoying the familiar sights and smells. The journey back had been easy, and just as Peter had promised, no time had passed there while they were in Neverland. London was still dark. The candles still flickered in the lampposts, and the air was damp as the last of the storm faded. Everything was almost the same. And yet, Wendy realized, she was so very different.

Hearing a sound, she turned and saw her mother coming out of her own room, pulling a shawl around her shoulders.

"Oh, goodness, Wendy, you gave me a fright," said her mother.

"Mother—I'm so sorry, Mother," Wendy said, as though their earlier fight had only just happened.

Mrs. Darling smiled and opened her arms wide. Like when she was a child, Wendy raced into them and wrapped her own arms tight around her mother's waist. She rested her head on

her mother's shoulder, surprised that they were nearly the same height now.

"There, there, my sweet girl." Mrs. Darling hushed her, gently running a hand over Wendy's hair. "It's quite all right."

"Mother, I think I'm ready," Wendy said, her words muffled by her mother's shoulder.

"Ready for what?" Mrs. Darling asked.

Wendy gulped. She knew that it was the right thing to do. Still, once she spoke the next words, there would be no going back. But then she thought of Peter and Hook and all the time they had lost getting hung up on the past. It was time she moved on.

"I'm ready to—" she started.

A thump from behind the nursery door interrupted her. It was followed by muffled voices.

Mrs. Darling pulled back. "Did you hear something?"

Wendy tried to look innocent. "No, I don't think so. . . ."

But then there was another thump, and this time, Mr. Darling popped his head out the bedroom door.

"Shhh!" he hissed at his daughter. "Do you hear that? Intruders!"

Wendy shook her head. "I don't hear anything at all. . . ."

Her parents ignored her and cautiously moved down the hall. Wendy sighed and followed. She had been hoping for a bit more time.

Pushing open the nursery door, Mr. and Mrs. Darling let out

surprised gasps as they came face to face with a roomful of children. Curly, Slightly, Nibs, Tootles, Bellweather, Birdie, and the twins were all there, their eyes wide as John and Michael showed them their toys. A few were bouncing on the beds, and Nibs was barking at Nana, who barked back, happy to be in the middle of so many kids.

"Who are all these children?" Mrs. Darling said, finally finding her voice.

The Lost Boys stopped bouncing and playing. Slowly, they moved forward, drawn to Mrs. Darling and her kind face and soft voice.

"Where on earth did you come from?" Mr. Darling asked as the children crowded around Mrs. Darling, each eager to get as close to a mother as possible.

"They came from Neverland, Father!" Michael said.

"Neverwhere?" Mr. Darling said, confused.

Before he could get an answer, Bellweather walked over and handed him his pocket watch. A bit worse for the wear, it was, nevertheless, ticking. He had fixed it! Mr. Darling looked down at the watch and back at the boy, then shook his head in bewilderment.

"What happened to my poor watch?" Mr. Darling asked.

"It's kind of a long story," said John.

Watching her parents and the children get to know one another, Wendy smiled. She had known her parents would be

welcoming to the children. That was why she had told Peter to leave everyone there. In time, they would try to return the kids to their own homes or find them new ones, but for now, the children could have a good sleep and a few warm meals, and maybe even a story from her mother.

Wendy turned and tiptoed from the room. There was one thing left to do. It was time to say goodbye. She climbed the stairs and made her way out onto the roof. Peter sat in shadow, perched on the shingles with Tinker Bell hovering by his side. Above them, the *Jolly Roger*, tethered to the chimney by a long length of rope, floated in the gentle night breeze. As she got closer, Wendy heard an unmistakable sound.

"Boy," she said softly, going over to him, "why are you crying?"

Peter looked up and rubbed his eyes. When they had first met, he would have made up an excuse. But that time was past. They were true friends now—and true friends told each other the truth.

"You know how you asked me where I came from?" he finally said.

"Yes . . ." Wendy said. It was the one question that had been left unanswered—until now.

Peter gestured to the chimney. As Wendy watched, Tinker Bell flew to it and lit up the bricks with her fairy glow. Wendy gasped as the light revealed a name carved into the bricks: *PETER PAN*.

"*This* was your home?"

Peter nodded. He took a breath and then told the story he had never before told anyone, ever. Not even Hook. "My mother scolded me one night and told me to grow up. And instead, I climbed out the window, leapt over the garden wall, and never looked back."

"Except you did," Wendy said, the whole picture suddenly becoming clear. "That's why you keep coming back. Because you miss your home."

Peter shrugged. "It's not my home anymore. It's yours," he said. "And I'm just a story—a story I told to any child who would listen...."

"Like my mother?" Wendy guessed.

Peter nodded. "And her mother before her. It never had an ending... until now." He paused. "Maybe I could still come back to listen to it sometime."

Wendy heard the longing and the sadness in Peter's voice, and it broke her heart. He had brought the Lost Boys home, but now he would be alone again. Sitting down next to him, Wendy tucked her nightgown in around her legs and then smiled at Peter gently.

"Or you could stay," she suggested.

"Here?" he asked.

"Yes."

"But you're going to leave," Peter pointed out. "You're going to grow up."

"You know, Peter, after all this, I think"—she paused to find the words—"that to grow up . . . might just be the biggest adventure of all."

Tears spilled down Peter's cheeks as he listened to her. Wendy wanted to reach out and comfort him. This boy, who was not afraid of pirates, was struck weak by the idea of being a grown-up.

"I don't think I'm ready," he said.

"Do you still have my kiss?" she asked.

Peter nodded and held up the thimble.

Taking it from him, Wendy looked down at the small object that carried so much meaning. Then she looked back up at Peter.

"May I give you one more?" she asked softly.

"Okay," Peter said. He held out his hand, waiting.

But instead of giving him another thimble, Wendy leaned forward and placed the softest, gentlest of kisses on his cheek. It was innocent and pure but full of unspoken feelings and promises.

Pulling back, she felt the wind cool her own cheeks and saw the surprise in Peter's eyes. "I guess we all grow up in our own time. And you've helped me find mine." She got to her feet, then held out her hand and helped Peter to his. "Go now. Come back when you're ready. And when you do . . . maybe you'll come find me."

Peter stood there, his mouth open as though he wanted to say yes. But before he could, a gust of wind caught the sail of the *Jolly Roger*, tugging it forward. The ship strained against

the chimney, and then, with a smash, the brick crumbled. Much of the chimney was yanked off the roof. Free of its holding, the ship began to drift away.

Peter's eyes darted back and forth between the ship and Wendy, his expression torn. But then, with one last longing look, he leapt into the air and jumped aboard the ship.

Hearing a chime, Wendy looked over and saw Tinker Bell hovering next to her.

"Goodbye, Tink," she said to the little fairy. "Take care of Peter. And don't forget about me."

Tinker Bell moved closer, then leaned over and spoke into Wendy's ear. And this time, Wendy understood her perfectly.

"Thank you for hearing me, Wendy," she said, and then, after giving Wendy a swift kiss on the nose, she darted off after Peter and the ship.

Wendy watched them go as down in the nursery, Mr. and Mrs. Darling and the children did the same. Each one felt a different tug as the ship sailed over the London skyline. For the Lost Boys, there was sadness tinged with love and gratitude. Peter had given them a lifetime of adventure, and they would miss him. But they were ready for what was to come. For the Darling parents, the ship brought a wisp of nostalgia, a gentle tug at a forgotten memory.

"What sort of magic is this?" Mr. Darling said softly. "Who is that boy?"

Beside him, Mrs. Darling stared out at the ship. And then, as if a dream had come back into focus, she knew. She had seen this ship. She had met this boy. It had been long ago, when she was just a girl. But she knew him.

"Why, that's Peter Pan," she told her husband as another gust of wind drifted through the night air and caused the glittering sails to billow. She squeezed her husband's hand and then looked at the children. What a magical night it must have been. . . .

Up on the roof, Wendy watched as the ship flew farther and farther into the night, its course set for the second star on the right. She could just make out Peter standing at the helm with his hat tilted jauntily on his head and Tinker Bell at his side.

As if sensing her gaze on him, Peter turned and ran to the edge of the deck. He held his hand up and stayed there as the ship moved away. The last glimpse she had of the boy was as the ship crossed in front of the moon, a perfect silhouette, a dreamy vision.

And then, just like that, it vanished into the night. All that was left were the twinkling stars and the bright moonlight. Wendy watched for a long time after the ship was gone, imagining it and its lone two crew members making their way back to a land like no other. It would be different without the Lost Boys and Hook, but Wendy had a feeling Peter had a few surprises up his sleeve.

Finally turning from the sky, she looked around at the city right in front of her. It seemed different somehow, softer, more magical. The streets seemed wider, the city more open, as if it was full of possibility. Wendy sighed and then started to head inside. But as she did, her gaze fell on Peter's name, etched into the remains of the chimney. She paused. The name was so small, and yet Peter Pan was larger than life—a story she hoped to tell her children and their children someday. But she had changed his story. He had said so himself. She had given it an ending. Walking to the remains of the chimney, she held up the kiss she had given Peter. She began to scratch at the brick with the thimble. When she was done, she stepped back and smiled.

Pleased with her work, she finally moved toward the house. It was time to check on the children—and her parents.

Behind her, a cloud passed over the moonlight. When the cloud cleared the moon, the bright light illuminated the chimney, revealing what had been scratched into the brick—the end of one story, and perhaps the beginning of a new one: *PETER PAN & WENDY*.

EPILOGUE

Another day dawned brightly over Neverland. In the hills, a warm breeze blew the green grass, making it ripple like water. Down in the pools at the shore's edge, the mermaids played, leaping and diving in the cool blue sea.

Then, out of the sea, something emerged. An arm, lacking a hand, burst into the air and grabbed hold of the nearest object—an overturned dinghy.

It was Hook!

Sputtering and panting, Hook pulled himself onto the overturned boat. He was soaked to the bone—his face blue and his fingers like prunes—but alive! He was most definitely alive.

He saw Smee clinging to a piece of rigging bobbing in the water some distance away. The man's legs were floating up in the air as he giggled with abandon.

"Captain!" he shouted, seeing Hook. "Did you see me, Captain?"

"Yes, I see you!" Hook shouted back, pulling a piece of

seaweed out of his shirt. "Right yourself and we might make it to shore yet!"

Smee nodded, but he was still focused on his fun. "But did you see me?" he said. "I flew! I really flew!"

A distant sound caused Smee to stop talking. Both he and Hook turned and looked to the horizon. They waited, their breath held, for the sound to come again.

"Did you hear that?" Hook asked.

Then he heard it again as a shadow passed over this head. He smiled. No, it wasn't the squawk of gulls. It wasn't even the terrifying ticktock of the crocodile. It was a sound he had been hearing his whole life. It was Tinker Bell, chiming Peter's return to Neverland. Hook looked up in the sky just as the *Jolly Roger* came into view. And for the first time in many years, Hook felt joy.

As the boat dipped lower, he saw Peter on the deck, with Tinker Bell hovering just ahead of him. Her golden light radiated over Neverland, and as they passed over Hook's dinghy, Peter reached down and pulled him aboard the ship.

Then, together, friends once more, they sailed toward the beaches of Neverland, ready for the new adventures to come.